Sanitarium Magazine
Issue no. 48

*Thank you to all of our contributors, we couldn't
have done it without you.*

FACULTY MEMBERS

Dr. Sputnik
Dr. Muratori
Dr. Soldan
Dr. Algee
Dr. Marceau
Dr. Warra

Contents

ISSUE FORTY-EIGHT

Dear Reader,

Summer is a strange beast for the horror fan. Long days that lend themselves to BBQ's, summer holidays to foreign lands and relaxing with friends. In this period of sunshine (it's not been too bad in the UK) it's easy to forget that autumn and the depths of winter are on their way. I use this time to reflect on the past few months and look ahead to what is coming.

We have the stand out "Don't Breath", the re-imagining of Stephen King's IT and the Blair Witch sequal to name a few. So enjoy the last weeks of summer and we hope you enjoy our selection of stories we have for you this issue.

Barry Skelhorn

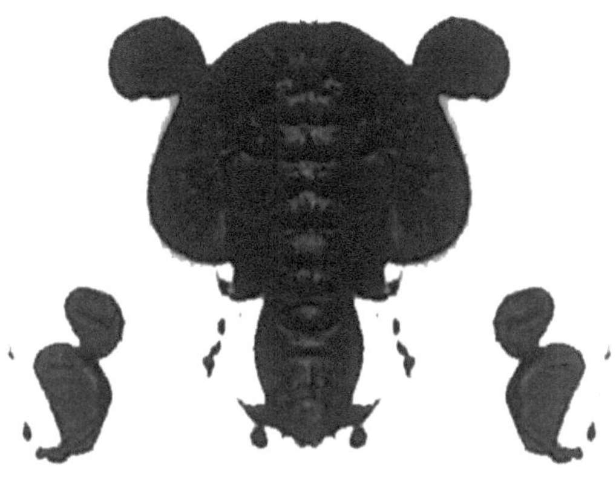

The Girl Next Door by Scott Cameron

I needed a change. I wanted to reinvent myself. I had to start from scratch; new town, new career and new friends. When I was offered a journalism job three cities over, it's safe to say I'd packed before I'd even had time to sign the contract. The excitement was overpowering. It felt like I was beginning a new chapter. In hindsight, you could say that I had viewed the move with rose tinted glasses, my mind throwing together images of opulence and scenarios where everything went in my favour. This dream started to shatter the moment I arrived at my new home. I had to choose the first place I could find, having only 2 weeks until my new job started and being restricted by a very modest income. The pictures that had been posted online must have been taken on a good day as, in the light of reality, the crumbing entry and the graffiti covered door did little to make this feel like the stunning bachelor pad I had envisioned.

I pushed open the door, taking care to avoid its cracked window pane, and walked into the reception area. The air was hot and humid, the summer heatwave turning most buildings into makeshift saunas. The room was split down the middle with an aged wooden counter which would have looked antique if not for the crude mesh wiring that rose from the wood to the ceiling. Nicotine coloured tiles covered the walls, amplifying every sound and causing every step to herald my arrival to anyone nearby. I walked up to the counter and pressed the little bell that was nailed to it. A brutish man stomped out from the room behind.

'Yeah?' he snorted. His frame and demeanour combined to create an imposing aura.

'I'm here about the apartment,' I said. 'My name's James Foley. I called a few days ago.' Rather than acknowledge what I said, the man turned around and ambled over to a cabinet in the back, then pulled out a bundle of papers from the battered metal drawer.

'You need to fill out these. I want 2 months rent up front. You do a runner, you lose your money,' he said. I didn't like his tone. I looked down at the contract. It was fairly basic, just a few standard comments about noise levels and drugs, neither of which I was partial to. I signed each page, taking great care not to touch the various stains on the paper and then I begrudgingly handed over an envelope with a large chunk of money. He grabbed the money and threw a set of keys in my general direction.

'Aren't you going to count that?' I asked.

'Nah. If it's wrong I know exactly where you'll be. Your room's on the second floor at the end of the hall. 203.' He didn't say goodbye or even thanks. He just strode off into a back room, having obviously met his quota for human interaction for today. I glanced over to the lift, a rusty metal box that wouldn't have surprised me if it was powered by a hand crank. I didn't want to use it, but the heat was sapping my strength and the thought of climbing two flights of graffiti ridden stairs appealed even less. I pressed the button and the old, copper-stained doors screeched open to reveal what could quite possibly be my final resting place. I stepped into the lift and the carriage dipped, straining under my weight, the wires used to suspend it protesting over the additional load.

'Excuse me! Do you mind if I jump on too?' said the old man that had managed to sneak up behind me. His choice of words did nothing to ease my tension. He shuffled onboard while struggling to carry several shopping bags, the extra load caused the entire contraption to scream. I felt nauseous. My mind devised vicious scenes where the lift gave in to the strain and failed, dropping our helpless frames into oblivion. Despite the various doom visages, I felt sorry for the frail old man and couldn't pluck up the nerve to leave.

'Which floor, sir?' I asked in a voice that was far more formal than intended.

'Oh, first floor please.' Even though his movements were strained and stiff, he had a large smile plastered across his aged face. I pressed the buttons for the first and second floors and the doors began to close.

'I'm James,' I said, trying to take my mind off the death trap I had just locked myself inside of. 'I'm moving into 203 today.'

'Ah, well hello to you. I'm Eli,' he said, shaking my hand energetically.

'So, 203 eh? You'd be the third person in as many months.'
'Why so many?' I asked, unsure if I wanted to hear the answer.
'Well who knows for sure but lets face it, we don't exactly live in a palace. Some people are always looking for something better. Maybe they thought this place was beneath them. Personally, I prefer to live within my means.' The bell sounded to signal our arrival on the first floor and the doors ground open to reveal a

corridor that seemingly appeared to be designed for the sole purpose of sensory deprivation. The hall was spartan. The walls were covered in an aged cream paint, their most remarkable feature being that they were completely unremarkable. There were three apartments on this level. Each door was made of cheap varnished wood with the numbers stuck on in a way that wouldn't look out of place on a wheelie bin. There were no windows in the hallway, the only light coming from a flickering, fluorescent tube that was clearly on it's way out. Eli stepped out, keys in hand, ready to finish his journey.

'Do you need a hand with those bags?' I asked.

'Oh, don't worry about that. I may look like a withered old fart but I'm stronger than I look,' he chuckled to himself. 'Come see me when you get settled and I'll make you a cup of tea. It would be nice to have a visitor.' And on that note, he disappeared into the first room.

The hall on the second floor was an exact copy of the previous floor, even down to the flickering light. It wouldn't have been a big stretch of imagination to see someone getting disorientated because they didn't pay attention to the floor they were getting off at. If I hadn't have already met Eli, it would have been difficult to see anyone else living here as, aside from the buzzing of the strip light, the hall was completely silent. I stepped out of the lift, feeling immediate relief to have escaped the confines of the lift and be back on solid ground. My new home was at the end of the corridor, exactly where the attendant said it would be. I slid the key into the lock and opened the door.

The apartment was unveiled like a prize in the shittiest contest ever. The main living room contained a desk, a lamp, half of a curtain and a phone that would have looked dated in the 80's. The floor was coated in cheap linoleum that had seen it's fair share of traffic. A large window allowed light to flood into the room, a welcome change from the claustrophobic atmosphere of the hallway. A crude partition separated the living room and the kitchen, which contained nothing but basic appliances that were at least a decade old. The bathroom was small but serviceable. A vent in the bottom of the wall meant that the room felt cool, which was a huge bonus during the heat wave I was having to endure. Lastly I checked the bedroom. Half a broken bed and a rickety chest of drawers that wouldn't have looked out of place in a dusty antique store.

A van with my possessions arrived later that afternoon. The driver didn't fancy taking the lift either so we braved the stairs, travelling up and down them for over an hour. There wasn't a lot of stuff but I didn't trust leaving it unattended so we took turns taking boxes up to my room. The guy was kind enough to take away the remains of the bed as I had luckily packed an air bed to be safe. Even considering the setting, having my stuff there made it feel immediately more like home. I didn't have a TV or an internet connection so I decided to play some rock on my laptop while I organised my belongings.

The move had worn me out but my stomach told me that food was a priority. I had no idea where the closest shop was so I decided to get it out of the way before it got dark. I stepped out into the hall and stood there for several moments while my eyes adjusted to the artificial light. It was a depressing place to be. I eased the door shut to avoid making too much noise. I hadn't met any of the other residents on this floor and didn't want my first interaction with them to be a negative one. I felt the latch click into place.

I had spent far more time than I had intended on my hunt for food. After walking round in circles for what seemed like an eternity, I stumbled across a small corner shop. The selection of food was slim, so I was forced to settle on chocolate bars, energy drinks and cake. Hardly the grown-up meal I had planned on for my first night in my new place. After picking up a few magazines to pass the time, I rushed back to my lair in order to begin my sugar-filled culinary journey.

The floor to my place quickly resembled a student dorm with empty cans and wrappers everywhere. Rather than do the grown-up thing and tidy, I decided to use the time less wisely and talked to my parents on the phone. They gave the usual speech about how much they would miss me and how proud they were that I had got a new job. My mother gave me a few cautionary tales about women with loose morals, and then my father typically took the other approach and encouraged me to 'get myself some'. Listening to my parents talk about sex was always a grim experience so I made my excuses and hastily ended the call. After chatting to a few close friends and then scribbling down a plan of action for tomorrow, I began to experience a sugar crash. My deluxe inflatable bed started to look very appealing and at the grand old time of 9.43pm I decided on sleep.

I woke up at 1.03am to the sound of sobbing. I sat up confused and allowed my eyes to adjust to the dark. My mind drank in my surroundings, creating various twisted sources in order to answer the question of the foreign noise. The sound was muffled but loud, suggesting that it wasn't coming from my room but was definitely close by. I silently got to my feet and allowed my sense of hearing to guide me through the dark. I gripped the door handle, my palms damp with perspiration and slowly opened the door to the living room, listening as the sound of sobbing grew louder. The room was lighter than the bedroom due to the amber glow of the street lights which poured through the window, leaving all but the corners of the room viewable. I began to shiver. The hairs on my arms and the back of my neck stood to attention. The air felt heavy and my whole body was on alert, as if someone was watching me, their gaze unwavering. I tentatively moved around the room in an attempt to eliminate any possible hiding place for my stalker. Then I saw it. Light coming from underneath the bathroom door.

I felt sick. My limbs felt weak and sweat trickled down my cheek. I struggled to catch my breath as I approached the sound. I could tell that behind the door was the source of the sobbing. I reached for the handle and dared myself to open it. Each time that I counted to three and each time I stood there, motionless. I stood there for what seemed like an eternity, listening with my ear to the door. I counted several more times, each time feeling as though I had enough courage to open it and each time my conviction failed.

'Hello? Who's there?' I enquired while trying to muster the most intimidating voice possible. My fear was apparent. The sobbing stopped.

'You can hear me?' a female voice replied meekly. The sound of her voice dissolved most of my fear and I plucked the courage to open the door. The bathroom was empty. I was about to freak out when the voice called out again.

'I take it you have just moved in? I'm sorry to have bothered you.' The voice was coming from the vent at the bottom of the wall. I felt like an idiot for not thinking about that option.

'It's ok. I couldn't really sleep. New place and all. My name is James. I live in 203.' There was a brief pause.

'I live next door,' she whispered. Her voice was still shaky from crying.

'Is something wrong?' I said, realising the absurdity of attempting to be a shoulder to cry on through an air vent.

'It's nothing. I'm sorry to have bothered you.' There was a sound of shuffling and then silence. I called out the her but she had gone. I was more than a little confused by the events that had just unfolded. Why was she so upset? I pondered many things as I ambled my way back into bed. Why was I even putting so much thought into this? Maybe it was a curiosity of the unknown. I didn't know her story, her appearance or the reasoning behind her sorrow. It was this unknown that sent my brain into a storm of ideas. My subconscious created various backstories to fill in the blanks. Sleep didn't come anytime soon.

The next day I managed to find a real supermarket and successfully managed to perform a sensible shop without blowing my money on energy drinks and donuts. The sun was intense, putting extra strain on my body as I carried several bulky bags down the long road to my home. Drenched in sweat, shaky from lactic acid and looking like I'd been swimming, I eventually made it back to my hall. The buzzing of the tube light had become almost welcoming and the lack of windows meant that the area was cool. My gaze turned to 202 as I walked along to my door. I considered knocking and introducing myself, but the sweat patches that had formed around my armpits were far from the best first impression that I wanted to give. That night I attempted to make a proper meal, or I would have done if the oven worked. My frustration was evident to anyone that may have overheard my long list of imaginative swear words and slamming of cutlery. I picked up the phone that was placed by the door and rang the cheerful man at reception. After several seconds he picked up.

'Yeah?' his tone once again sounded disinterested.

'Hi. It's James in 203.' I made every effort to sound cheerful.

'Yeah?' I could have sworn there was an echo.

'The oven doesn't appear to be working. Can you come and check it out?'

'Have you tried plugging it in?' he barked. 'It needs electricity to work.' I could feel my anger building up. I wasn't sure if he was deliberately trying to be insulting or if he was just an all round dick. I bit my tongue.

'Yes! I've done that. I just can't get anything to…' the sobbing started again. I didn't bother saying goodbye and just put the phone down. It was nearly dark but knowing where the sound originated from had done a lot to ease my overactive imagination. I walked into the bathroom and sat down next to the vent.

'Do you want to talk?' I asked. There was a short gasp.

'I'm sure you have your own things to worry about. I wouldn't want to bother you.' every couple of words were interrupted by a sniffle.

'You wouldn't be bothering me. I'm new to the area and don't really know anyone. It would be nice to talk to someone. Even through an air vent.' I realised as I said this that I sounded like a bit of a desperate loser. I could hear her trying to stifle a giggle. I tried to look through he vent to see if I could catch a glimpse of my mysterious acquaintance but all I could see was darkness.

'I shouldn't be talking. He might hear,' she said in a hushed voice.

'Who?' I asked.

'My husband. He doesn't like me talking to people.' There was the sound of a door slamming in the distance. 'I have to go.' That felt wrong. Should I be trying to help her? I considered storming next door like some kind of super hero to save her, but what if I have the wrong end of the stick? My mind tended to overreact and assume the worst.

I was woken up again that night. Not to the sound of the girl next door. This time it was tapping. Three slow deliberate taps coming from another room. I was tired. My head felt like it was too big for my body and my limbs felt like they were missing bones. I could only describe a feeling as though I'd been savagely beaten in my sleep. I strained to pull myself from my bed and staggered towards the bedroom door. I could hear my heart trying to break through my ribs and I struggled the catch my breath. I leant against the bedroom wall to support myself while I pried open the door. The tapping increased in intensity, sounding more like someone was trying to demolish a wall. It was coming from my front door. Each step I took towards the door seemed to increase the speed of the noise. The sound was deafening. I threw my agonised body towards the front door and as I made contact, everything stopped. I peered through the peephole, out into the familiar corridor but I couldn't see anything. I searched around looking for my keys and was interrupted by another bang from the door. I rushed back to look through the peephole. Something had changed. Opposite me I could see an object stuck to the wall. It was my keys.

My first instinct was to flee. I tried the front door but it was locked. I spun round. My eyes scanned the living room frantically. Someone had been in here! Someone was messing with my head! Each dark corner of the room served to fuel my nightmarish visions of some psychotic intruder lurking, waiting, stalking me. I watched the corners as I hugged the wall and inched my way towards the lamp that was on the desk in the far corner. I flicked the switch and the room was bathed in light. I was alone. I took a minute to catch my breath and allow myself to stop shaking. My home didn't feel safe. How the hell did someone get in? I needed to get out so I rushed to the bedroom to change and grab some things. As I opened the door, I reeled in horror. Every single wall was covered in hastily scrawled writing. Most of the words were illegible, mad scratchings, but then I saw something coherent just above where my head would be while I slept. I saw two words, "She's mine."

That was more than enough of an excuse for me to run. I didn't even grab a bag. I threw on the first clothes I could find and ran head first into the front door in a feral attempt to overpower the lock. I failed. I geared up for a second go, my shoulder protesting to any more punishment.

'James? Are you there?' The voice stopped me in my tracks. She spoke in that way people do that sounds like a whisper, but wasn't quieter in any way. I considered ignoring her. I was freaked out, scared and confused. Talking to a disembodied voice while sat next to my toilet wasn't going to make me feel any better about my current situation, but there was something about her voice that gave off panic. It was something I couldn't just ignore. I rushed to the vent in the bathroom.

'What's up?' I asked, sounding short of breath.

'It's my husband! He's watching you! Oh god help...' What followed could only be described as a scream of pure terror. I couldn't risk ignoring it. I ran into my front door, throwing all my weight into the wooden frame. It gave way easily, splinters of MDF covering the hall, my momentum barely phased by the act. I reached 202 and banged my fist on the door.

'Hello? Open the door!' I demanded. There was no reply. I couldn't believe what I was doing. My mind making me question what I'd heard. Another scream, much louder than the first, quashed any doubt in my course. I grabbed the handle and charged in to 202, adrenaline pumping through every muscle. But it was what I saw that stopped me in my tracks.

I saw nothing. The place was empty, no furniture, no body, no light aside from what was coming in through the open door I had just come through. The room looked like it had been burnt out, black stains covered the floor and walls. It clearly hadn't been lived in for several years. 'Hello?' I called out nervously. Almost as in response, the door I had entered through slammed shut. I rushed to it and tried to open it, but it wouldn't budge an inch. I tried running at it in panic, every instinct telling me that something was wrong. The door stood solid. I started to bang my fist on the door helplessly. Defeated, I spun round, my eyes unable to see anything in the now pitch-black room. The sobbing began again, so much clearer than before. In fact, no, it wasn't sobbing. It was laughing…

Finding somewhere to live that a student would call affordable was far from easy. I wasn't exactly loaded and studies meant that I couldn't work full-time, so I couldn't really be picky. I headed up the short steps and into the dirty, graffiti ridden hall. After signing the contract and handing over what seemed like a fortune to my bank balance, I was handed the key to room 203. As I headed towards the steps up to the second floor, I noticed an old man who had just entered, carrying several large bags.

'Do you need any help there, sir?' I asked

'That's very kind of you. I don't think I've seen you here before. I'm Eli,'

'Yes, I'm new here. I've just moved into 203. I'm Abigail.'

'203?' he asked quizzically, 'You're the fourth person in as many months.'

The End.

CASE #76341

THE GIRL NEXT DOOR
BY SCOTT CAMERON

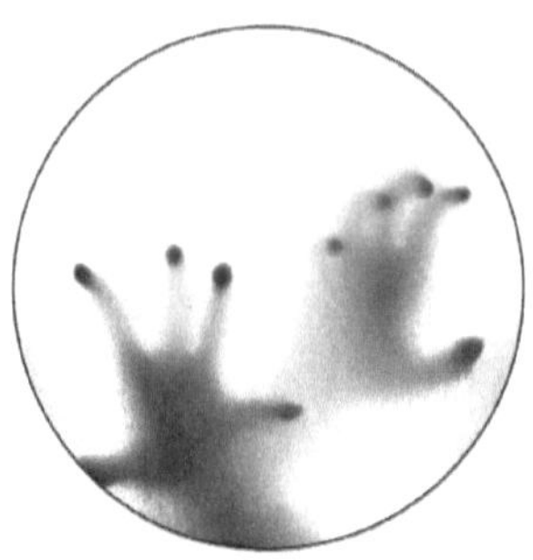

Scott Cameron lives in West Yorkshire (UK) and is a novice writer, who's main motivation is to make his 3 year old son proud. This is the first thing Scott has written, having given in to procrastination and countless nights staring at a blank page, waiting for that perfect first sentence. You can follow him on Twitter @SugoiScott

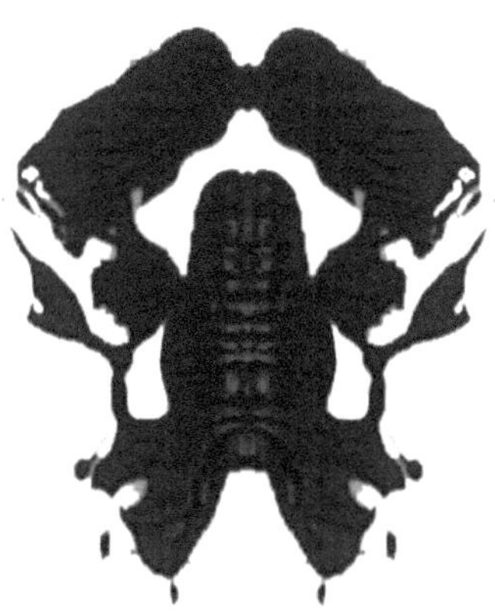

Shadows In The Dark by William Cook

The shadows in the dark, morph and move like liquid night. I can hear them whispering. I can hear them breathing. They surround my bed like crows around carrion – their black forms without definition, blurred beyond reason and shape. They move like memories – swelling, growing with each breath, then shrinking, receding, swallowed by the blackness until the night is still again and all I hear is the blood, pumping through my temples. Mother does not answer my cries anymore, so I have stopped crying out. I have learned to live with my fear, to accept that reality is nothing less than a waking nightmare. And each night they return. As the dusk dwindles and fades outside my bedroom window, as the last vestiges of light burn low and disappear between the cracks in the curtains, the shadows reappear. Their whispers start with a soft murmur, barely discernible at first, like the noise of a baby calf mewling, but as the night progresses, the whispers grow in intensity and volume until a 'whooshing' sound, much like the sound of a prairie wind buffeting the outer walls of our house, fills my room. I clasp my hands over my ears but the sound is in my mind. The sound fills my body, my heart fluttering beneath my ribs like a pillow-case on the clothesline in the wind. I stifle my cries, for some times I cannot contain my fear. It bursts from my body like a flock of pigeons on the wing.

The thin blanket on the bed affords a false security as I huddle beneath the fabric, praying to gods I don't believe in, wishing that the shadows would take their leave and go. But they don't. Since they first appeared six months ago, creeping from the wall corners and the ceiling of my room, they have steadily approached my bed. Stalking me with a slow agonizing advance. Inch by inch, the darkness comes. And now . . . now they stand over me. I feel their presence looming, hovering mere fractions above the blanket that covers my trembling body. I hold my breath, waiting for the inevitable touch – I imagine thick black coils of molasses, twisting and turning, spindly fingers as black as ink winding their way through my hair until they grip and yank me up into the dark black night, never to be seen again. But so far, the ultimate darkness eludes me – sleep holds no sanctuary and my mind keeps circling around the possibility, that death is the only way out.

The morning light slowly fills the room. The shadows have receded back into the corners, into the timber walls covered in peeling wallpaper, back under the bed, beneath the standing closet, under the chest of drawers . . . Weak with sleep deprivation I sit up. The old wire-frame mattress creaks beneath me, my breath mists in the frigid air as I gingerly extend one bare foot onto the cold timber floorboards, retracting it slightly before placing both feet firmly on the floor. I've given up checking for the shapeless darkness under the bed and in the cracks and corners – I know what I will see amongst the cob-webs and mice droppings, the smallest of shadows curled up in the recesses free from the harsh light of day. And there they'll stay, until night-fall, innocuous, almost indiscernible to the naked eye.

I yawn, shivering with the cold as I quickly pull a shirt over my head and buckle the belt holding up my jeans. I tug on some socks and tie my bootlaces before slipping my jerkin over my shoulders and my slouch hat on my head. I look around the room once more, chastising myself for my continued foolishness, and then open the door and step down onto the muddy ground. I leave the door wide open, hoping that the shadows will escape, that some force will extricate them from my dwelling before I return from the fields.

The early-morning earth is crisp and hard with frost as I trudge across the field to the furthest boundary of our property. We have mined these fields for nutrients for decades. My grandfather once worked these fields before he passed and handed on the property to my father. It is not a big plot of land, but big enough for us to have pulled a living from the soil each quarter; potatoes providing the main source of food and income for our family, for as long as I can remember. We'd had some livestock for a while; a couple of cows, a few pigs and some goats, but after a particularly nasty winter we lost most of them to the cold and they ended up on our dinner plates. Pa grew beets and radishes to alternate between the low-yielding months, but the crops had dwindled as his health failed and Mother's madness blossomed.

Harold, my older brother, had fled the farm only to return a year later with his 'tail between his legs' as Mother had described him. He lasted another three months before Pa found him hanging from the loft rafter in the barn. I remember him swinging there, so high up and lifeless, the rope creaking on the timber strut, as the breeze that blew through the cracks in the barn-wall, slowly rotated his body mid-air. I remember the thud when he hit the hay-bales that Pa had stacked beneath him. Pa wept with the sickle in his hand, standing up there in the loft, amongst the shadows. Harry lay spread-eagled atop the rancid hay-bales, one broken leg twisted beneath him, his head turned at a queer angle, his glazed eyes staring dead ahead and his blue tongue lolling from the corner of his mouth still open in an 'O.' I didn't cry for my brother because the shadows had started to come for me by then. Harry had taken the easy way out and left me for dead. At that point I loathed my brother, but now I understood him completely. I stopped turning the soil with the hoe and looked back across the field to the small house and the remains of the barn that stood off to one side. The blackened husk of the barn still defied gravity, despite Pa's best efforts to burn it to the ground. I remember the night he'd set it ablaze as if it were yesterday. I woke from a rare deep sleep, my small bedroom glowing a rich red-hued orange. I scratched the curtains back from the window-pane and recoiled at what I saw. I ran from my room outside and stopped, the intense heat pushing me back as huge flames licked the night sky above. Billowing clouds of smoke rose into the darkness as showers of embers floated all around like frenetic fire-flies. Mother sat on her knees, tearing clumps of her black hair from her scalp – moaning and rocking as she stared into the fire, her night-dress soiled with mud and god-knows-what.

I staggered to one side, edging around the barn, calling out for Pa. All I could hear was the roar of the blazing fire as it devoured the stored hay and the timber walls of the barn. Smoking ash floated all around me, embers tumbling in the updrafts created by the blaze, as I became consumed with a fear that hell had been unleashed upon our small family. A distant memory of the Sunday pastor's words filled my mind as he roared passages from Isaiah: "For, behold, the LORD will come with fire, and with his chariots like a whirlwind, to render his anger with fury, and his rebuke with flames of fire." We had sinned. My brother had sinned. My mother blasphemed at the drop of a hat and my thoughts were impure, oh so impure . . . I could hear Pa's screams then. Coming from the center of the blaze, an awful noise broke forth from the wall of fire. His screams were high pitched until the smoke and fire choked his last breath from his charred lungs. Pa emerged from the flames, a fiery form stumbling blindly, his burning arms outstretched stiff before him as his entire body was ravaged by the twisting inferno. He took a few more steps and stopped, framed by the gaping entrance churning with smoke and cinders. I watched in horror as his eyes burst from his skull and ran down his blistered cheeks like black tears, the viscous fluids momentarily extinguishing the flames that licked his face. He pitched forward onto the barn floor, smoke curling from his burnt body. Mother's howling screams intensified as she picked herself up and ran towards Pa's blackened corpse.

The flames seemed to reach out to her as she approached. Long tendril-like fingers of fire lashed her body as she fought her way through the flames and burning debris to collapse onto Pa's charred and lifeless body. She started screaming, in the same high-pitched way Pa had done just moments ago, as her night-dress exploded into flame and her hair was scorched from her peeling scalp. I dropped to my knees, stunned beyond belief – wondering if this were not just some sick dream that I was still in the midst of.

Above the smoke and the embers, rain began to fall and before long I was soaked to my skin. As the flames dissipated with the blanket of soft rain and the main body of the barn collapsed in a shower of sparks and ash, I wept. Mother and father were gone, just like Harold. The fire had eaten their souls and now the night was closing in again as the last of the flames turned to smoke. The pitter-patter rain sizzling on the glowing embers of the barn's skeletal remains.

I swallowed hard; tears flowed like the rain that ran in rivulets down my face. The next day I turned back to my work and the day after that. Months passed as I stabbed at the earth with the sharp end of the hoe until I could do no more. From the seed-bag that hung from my tired shoulders, I sowed the long ruts in the soil with new life, covering the last of the seeded-potato sprouts quickly with the turned soil. Burying them as I had my family, although these would grow again . . . hopefully. I turned and trudged back across the barren fields, between the arable land where I had sown the potato crop and the farm house and remains of the barn. I stopped before I reached the front door, steadying myself as I swayed in the wind that now ripped across the plains. A long mare's tail of black cloud filled the grey sky, looming ominously above. I looked out beyond our property, miles away the low flat-hills and mesas sat hunched like coyotes waiting for prey but nothing else remained to be seen. Like an endless ocean, the barren fields and plains stretched for as far as the eye could see and I felt terribly alone. More alone than I had ever felt in my life. Twenty-three years gone Friday and I had nothing to show for the passing of my time.

I coughed a spittle of blood into my fist and opened my parched mouth to breathe deeply. We had no water since the fire and the last rain – three long months of rationed tank water and now nothing. The only fluid left on the property was the quarter of potato broth perched on the iron stove in the living room of the farmhouse. I removed my jerkin and dropped it on the porch step, my shirt billowing around me like a boat-sail. The weather had now turned and a warm breeze blew strong across the fields, signaling the approach of spring and the summer months to come. The cold frosty nights of the desert plains had been enough to collect some moisture on the angled corrugated iron that I used to syphon meagre, but precious, drops of condensation, but that was about to end.

I sighed a hollow breath and dropped to one knee. I was exhausted, my hands were raw and my skin burnt from the elements despite my layers of clothing. I had open sores and wounds that wouldn't heal and my hair fell out in clumps on my stained pillow each morning. I was in bad shape and I knew that I didn't have long to go. Both mother and father had sacrificed their food rations for me until their hunger could contain their frugality no longer. The hunger drove Ma crazy, Pa said. We had lived off the skinny horse that pulled the cart to market for as long as we could. But the meat went bad and made us all sick. Despite the sickness, the meat had been a welcome change from the vegetable broth that we ate morning and night, and when it was gone and buried in the ground, I feared the worse. We tried not to notice the proud ribs that jutted through our clothes like the slats on a washboard. We tried not to notice the sunken cheeks and rotting teeth of each other – the skeletal limbs that still managed to turn the soil and gather the pathetic crops. We were dying slowly, miserably, and so the flames would've held their appeal to my parents, I guess. The flames weren't for me.

This day, I could work no more. Barely able to stand, I looked hopelessly around the bare interior of the dilapidated farmhouse. The last of the tinder sat in the open stove, no flint or match-wood to be had, despite the charred remains of the barn laying useless in the field. I managed to stand, my head spinning with fatigue and hunger, yet still I walked out the front door and around the side of the house to the dead tree in the back yard where I finally collapsed. The day's light was waning, the sun now sunk beyond the low-lying ranges in the distance. The shadows rolled in across the plains like an advancing army.

I lay face down in the dirt. I slowly reached out my skinny arms and scooped the dusty earth up in each hand. One for my mother, one for my father, none for my coward brother. The grave mounds had sunk beneath the surface now – the earth cracked and lifeless where they lay beneath, scorched and blackened shells. Both of them lay side by side, Ma and Pa – my brother's bones lay to the left of my mother. I crawled with the last of my strength and lay next to my father's side, rolling onto my back. I looked through the spindled dead limbs of the tree above me and saw the first twinkling stars appear in the night sky. I shivered as the cold closed in but remained where I lay. My hunger had gone, replaced with an unbearable hollowness that seemed to fill my thin carcass with its nothingness. The whispers began as the shadows crept closer. The prairie wind picked up and the air whistled through the burnt remains of the barn timbers in the near distance. I watched the stars slowly disappear as the shadows swelled and grew, the smell of burnt timber still lingering in my nostrils despite the passing of months. The whispers rose in volume. The now familiar whooshing noise of the shadows in the dark filled the silence, as words floated around me in the dark.

I could hear my brother's voice calling me from the shadows. I could hear my mother's voice, clear and strong like before she got the sickness. My father urged me to follow their voices, to follow the shadows in the night so we could be together once again. And so I did. I let the darkness come into me as the shadows filled my being and for the longest while I slept, with not a care in the world.

The End.

CASE #60281

SHADOWS IN THE DARK
BY WILLIAM COOK

William Cook was born and raised in New Zealand and is the author of the popular psychological thriller, 'Blood Related' and editor of 'Fresh Fear: An Anthology of Macabre Horror.' He is also the author of two non-fiction books: 'Gaze Into The Abyss: The Poetry of Jim Morrison' and 'Secrets of Best-Selling Self-Published Authors.'

He has also written many short stories that have appeared in anthologies and has authored two short-story collections ('Dreams of Thanatos' & 'Death Quartet') and two collections of poetry ('Journey: the search for something' & 'Corpus Delicti'). William writes Psychological Thrillers mostly, but also dabbles in Horror Fiction and, more recently, Non-Fiction.

He is currently hard at work on a sequel to his Psychological Thriller, 'Blood Related,' a second volume of 'Secrets of Best-Selling Self-Published Authors' and an exciting new Pulp Thriller Series all due out in 2016. Stay tuned!

Grab a free copy of William's 250 pg collection, 'Dreams of Thanatos.' Sign up now for the VIP newsletter at: http://williamcookwriter.com/p/subscribe-now.html (just copy and paste into your browser).

Member of the Australian Horror Writers Association, SpecFicNZ
& the SFFANZ.
Website http://williamcookwriter.com/

CASE #: 95425

As The Crow Flies by Krystal Lawrence

After a futile battle to hang onto her house amid a messy and bitter divorce, Brianna Douglas accepted the inevitable and allowed her wretched ex-husband to sell the marital residence and cash her out for her half.

After eight years of feeding the neighborhood birds and squirrels she hoped they would be able to adjust to the lack of birdseed, shelled peanuts and grain bread she left out for them on a daily basis. Her mother assured her that animals were very adaptable and they would make do without her. Brianna hoped that was true. She had offered to leave both the birdbath and feeder for the new owners, but they did not want them. Brianna couldn't help feeling guilty, as though she was letting the neighborhood wildlife down.

As is usually the case when a couple gets divorced, their friends picked a side. Few landed in Brianna's camp. It was understandable. Rob, her ex, had a mini-mansion boasting a movie theatre with surround-sound, and an Olympic size swimming pool complete with a skinny, topless supermodel named Ariel.

The only thing Rob hadn't fought for in the divorce was their cat, Bartholomew. Ariel was allergic to cats.

Brianna came from humbler means and returned to them after she and Rob broke up. During the eight years she was married she enjoyed the lavish lifestyle his income as a neurosurgeon provided, but once the divorce was final, she was just as happy to trade in the Mercedes she was awarded in the divorce for a nice sensible Subaru. She hadn't married Rob for his money, and only quit her job at his request when they were married. He wanted a stay-at-home domestic goddess, and that is just what Brianna had been for the duration of her married life.

The first year and a half or so was good. After that it was five years of contentious arguments, numerous other women, and one embarrassing sexually transmitted disease Rob brought home and never told her about. She had to find out she had contracted it the hard way——by experiencing the entire gamut of appalling symptoms. It was the chlamydia that finally drove Brianna to take the cat and leave.

After a hellish year of attorneys, unreasonable settlement demands, and Rob's frantic attempt to transfer all his holdings to offshore bank accounts before the judge froze his assets, the divorce was at last final. The courts were generous and Brianna was awarded a healthy settlement, including a very comfortable monthly alimony.

Later in the day, after the judgment had been rendered, Rob left a scathing and profane message on Brianna's voicemail. He claimed the judge who presided over their divorce was a lesbian, and implied that Her Honor and Brianna were involved in a sordid relationship—— the details of which, he described in most colorful and graphic terms. Numerous and increasingly threatening messages punctuated the next three months of Brianna's life, until her lawyer filed a restraining order to force Rob to stop calling.

It came as little surprise when after only six months Rob took her back to court to have the alimony reduced. He had yet to send her one check on time, and two months he never sent it at all.

Rob lost this battle, prompting another round of vicious and screaming phone messages, followed by an injunction levelled against him and a steep fine imposed by the judge. Brianna had a very good lawyer.

While she left the marriage far from poor, Brianna could not afford, nor did she desire, another huge house in a pretentious neighborhood. She settled for a comfortable three-year-old Colonial in a nice, well-maintained community on the other side of town. She bought the house because of the beautifully manicured and fenced backyard. It had mature trees, lush foliage and a covered patio suitable for her favorite pastime—— birdwatching. An amateur ornithologist, Brianna came to love all the different species who visited the feeder in her old home. She was anxious to make the acquaintance of the birds in her new neighborhood.

Upon getting settled, the first thing Brianna did was set up the bird feeder and begin a morning ritual of toasting grain bread and scattering it on the lawn in her backyard.

Within a week, three crows began waiting each morning for Brianna to arrive with the toast. She would enjoy her coffee on the patio while the crows came to nibble on the bread. She spoke to them, and they cawed conversation in return.

After two weeks of settling into this routine, Brianna was surprised to find a small and very pretty Abalone shell on the edge of her patio one morning. She knew at once that the crows had left it for her. When she picked it up, she saw one of the crows watching her intently from the top of the fence. "Did you give this to me?" she asked him.

The crow cawed once and bobbed its head.

Wow, thought Brianna. It was almost as though he understood what she asked and had nodded in the affirmative.

"Well, thank you. It's lovely."

Not long after that, about once a week Brianna would receive a small gift or trinket on her patio from the crows. There was a broken bit of stained glass once, a few coins, a couple seashells, and once an actual gold ring with a jade-colored stone that was quite beautiful. The birds seemed to like shiny objects, and from Brianna's point of view they had pretty good taste. She put the stained glass piece up in the garden window in her kitchen. Everything else she saved in a keepsake box she bought just for the gifts the crows bestowed upon her.

As the season changed and the weather grew warmer, Brianna took up jogging. She became friendly with a few people who lived on her block. She got to know Bobby and Renee Christopher, the couple who lived next door. They always complimented Brianna on how beautiful her garden was. They noticed the numerous birds always visiting Brianna's feeder or perched in the trees in her yard.

Brianna liked the couple, and one day invited Renee over for a glass of wine in the late afternoon.

As the two women sat chatting on Brianna's patio, a large flock of birds twittered loudly and rose up en-masse from a pine tree at the back of Brianna's yard. They fluttered off into the horizon.

Renee gasped and put a hand to her chest. "Good lord, that was like a scene right out that Hitchcock movie. Don't all those birds creep you out just a little?"

Brianna was taken aback by the question. "No, not at all. I love the birds. Especially my crows. I have three that come for breakfast every morning."

Renee Christopher wrinkled her nose. "Ew! Crows? They are such nasty things. Aren't they supposed to be a bad omen or something?"

To bring the point home she raised a gold cross she wore around her neck and held it up, as if to ward off the evil birds.

Brianna, sounding slightly amused, replied, "I believe you have them confused with vampires. They are actually incredibly smart birds." "Well, I don't like them. As long as they stay on your side of the fence." Renee laughed uncomfortably and drained her wine glass.

As Renee rose to leave, Brianna was startled to see two of the crows perched in her pink Dogwood tree watching her neighbor with bright-eyed interest. They did not shift their gaze until the woman had disappeared inside her back door.

Brianna asked, "Did you guys hear that? Don't worry about it. Your breed just has a bad rap, that's all. Want some peanuts, guys?" She shook some from a bag onto the lawn before going inside.

Three days later Brianna found a present at the edge of her patio. It was a gold necklace that looked suspiciously like the cross Renee Christopher had been wearing.

Brianna picked it up and bounced it on her palm. *No, it can't be,* she thought. She looked around her yard, but the crows were nowhere to be seen. She carried the cross inside and placed it in the keepsake box.

The following week as she was just leaving for her run, Renee flagged her down. Brianna stopped to see what her neighbor wanted. She was only a little surprised when Renee asked, "You haven't seen a gold cross lying around anywhere have you? I lost mine."

Brianna told her she hadn't, but that she would keep an eye out for it when she was out jogging. She pondered the situation. She knew crows were smart, but were they really smart enough to over-hear a conversation and get offended enough to steal someone's jewelry? She didn't think so. Brianna reasoned that it had to be a coincidence. Renee must have dropped the necklace outside somewhere and one of the crows found it. They left it for Brianna, just as they had the other items frequently placed on the patio for her. While the cross wasn't as sparkly as most of the items the crows seemed to favor, this was not the first piece of jewelry to show up on her patio.

Brianna waited a couple of days before placing the cross on Renee's front porch in a conspicuous location where she knew it would be found.

That same morning, while the crows nibbled at the toast she put out, she told them, "Hey, don't steal the neighbor's stuff anymore. Even if you don't like her. Capiche?"

***

Having lost his last attempt at having Brianna's alimony lowered, Rob tried again six months later. Frustrated and still paying off the legal fees from her divorce, Brianna sat on her patio in tears reading the court summons. She explained the situation to her sister on the phone and wept bitterly about having to endure another costly legal battle with her greedy ex-husband. Sometimes it seemed like this nightmare would never end.

After hanging up the phone with her sister, Brianna watched the crows as they picked at the bread. She asked, "How do you guys do it? How do you mate for life? We humans try, but I married a bastard who I feel like I will be fighting with for the rest of my life. Damn Rob Douglas and his anorexic super-model too," she spat, slamming her hand down hard enough on the patio table to startle two chickadees into flight from the birdfeeder.

The largest of the three crows paused with a piece of toast in his mouth. With his head titled sideways, he looked curiously at Brianna for a long moment before cawing to his mates and returning his attention to the bread.

A few days later when Brianna went out to fill the birdfeeder, she noticed something odd. There was a pattering of red dots splashed across her patio and an item that she could not immediately identify lying where the crows always left her presents.

After filling the feeder with birdseed, Brianna knelt down to examine what the crows had brought her. It was lacking the usual shiny hue of most of their offerings, and for the first few seconds Brianna could not comprehend what she was seeing.

34

When she recognized it for what it was, Brianna gasped and shot to her feet. All of a sudden the red dots spattered across her patio made a very sick kind of sense. She backed away from the object and looked around for the crows. They were nowhere to be seen.

With a queasy stomach, Brianna went inside for a roll of paper towels. She wasn't going to touch what she had just found with her bare hands.

Donning kitchen gloves, she gingerly rolled it onto a paper towel and disposed of it in the waste can kept by the side of the house.

The crows had left her a human finger.

Brianna went inside and washed her hands. She shuddered, wondering if someone wasn't looking for the thing, wanting to reattach it to the hand from which it had been severed. She wondered where the crows could have possibly found such a bizarre entity. She assumed the digit must have been separated by some type of tractor or industrial accident in a field or on a farm somewhere. She knew these things happened occasionally. Brianna had once dated a man whose mother mowed off three of her toes with a power lawnmower many years ago. Of course, this happened in the backwoods of Arkansas. Brianna rather doubted that type of thing happened very often here in the suburbs of Southern California.

The question was: Why would the crows think a severed finger would make a nice gift for her? How did they graduate from sparkly seashells and odd bits of jewelry to this?

Okay, she thought. *Now it's creepy.*

Later that day, she rented a pressure washer and set to work cleaning the blood spatter from her patio. As she fired up the washer the crows watched and cawed at her from the Dogwood. In a hushed tone she muttered, "Don't bring me anymore body parts, okay birdies?"

After removing the blood, she went inside and carried Bartholomew away from the window where he always sat to watch the birds in the yard, while making what she called his bird-voice——a strange clicking sound that was nothing at all like his normal meow. She closed the curtains, cutting off both of their views of the yard. She didn't feel like looking at the birds——and especially the crows today. She was having a little too much trouble digesting the nasty surprise they had left her.

***

Two months later, Brianna returned to court for the hearing on the reduction of her alimony. She felt a strange sense of déjà vu as she looked around the dismal courtroom. The entire experience was like visiting a movie set. Nothing had changed since the last time she was here, not even the players.

There was the painfully thin model; sitting behind Rob and constantly rubbing his shoulders and cooing in his ear, while simultaneously staring daggers at Brianna. And of course, her ex-husband; looking in ill-temper as he conferred with his counsel and absentmindedly batted the model's hand away. There was Rob's lawyer, Mr. Silverstein; looking through documents and whispering in his client's ear. And her own attorney, Paula; chewing on the end of a ballpoint pen and reviewing her notes.

Brianna did her best to ignore her ex. There were two attorneys between them——Rob's, extremely overweight, and blocking the view of her ex-husband quite nicely. She reminded herself that this would all be over soon, and she wouldn't have to come back to this miserable place again until Rob threw his next tantrum about the alimony. Paula had assured her the chances of the judge granting Rob's motion to have her support reduced were extremely unlikely.

The court was called to order and Rob's attorney rose to make his argument to the judge.

"Your Honor, my client has suffered a debilitating injury that has impacted his ability to perform his job. It will substantially decrease his earning capability for the foreseeable future. In light of this new circumstance, we must respectfully request that you grant our motion for a reduction in the amount of alimony Doctor Douglas pays, to an amount that will commensurate with his reduced income."

The judge replied, "I see. And exactly what is this debilitating injury your client has suffered, counselor?"

The attorney raised Rob's arm and showed the judge. "You see, Your Honor? The poor man has lost a finger on his left hand. It's been devastating for him."

Brianna's breath caught. All at once her heart began fluttering like the wings of the birds she loved so much. She was overcome by a jolting sense of vertigo and grasped the edge of the table to keep from listing sideways.

Her attorney, hearing Brianna's sharp intake of breath, placed her hand over her client's and patted it reassuringly. Paula whispered, "Stay cool, Bri."

The judge asked, "May I see the documentation which supports your claim of Doctor Douglas's reduced earnings please? I assume you have written confirmation from the treating physician that states he is no longer able to perform surgery."

The lawyer stumbled. "Err..well, Your Honor, I did not say my client was unable to operate on his patients. He can still do that, but he won't be performing nearly as many of these procedures as he did before he sustained such an egregious injury. Therefore, it stands to reason that his earnings will decrease."

Paula rose from the defense table, "Your Honor, we object to any change in alimony based on Doctor Douglas's assumption that his future earnings will be affected by his injury. Without proof that he is making less money at this time, we strongly object to this motion. While we are sorry for Doctor Douglas's unfortunate wound, I would like to note that he is right-handed, and the loss sustained was to his left. We believe this is nothing more than yet another attempt by the plaintiff to try and get out of his obligation to provide spousal support for Mrs. Douglas."

The judge smiled at Paula, and said, "I've got this, counselor. Objection noted."

Turning back to Rob's lawyer, she asked, "Mr. Silverstein, have you any documentation to show the court that substantiates your claim? Even Doctor Douglas's last paycheck stub will suffice. If his income has declined, it will be reflected there."

"Your Honor, I think the fact that he will be making less money should be obvious! He's a surgeon who is now handicapped! From which hand the finger is missing is completely irrelevant."

"So, I take it your answer is no? There is no proof. Is that correct?" The lawyer bellowed, "The proof is the man's horribly disfigured hand! You can clearly see that his finger is missing, can't you? What other

proof do you need, Judge?"

The judge's sunny disposition disappeared instantly. Her mouth thinned to a severe line. "You will want to watch your tone, counselor. You are just one outburst shy of sanctions."

Silverstein hastily apologized and returned to his seat.

The judge glared at Rob. "Doctor Douglas, it is this court's understanding that you have been consistently late in paying the previously ordered payments due your ex-wife. I am putting you on notice that going forward I am imposing interest compounded daily in the amount of twenty percent for each day Mrs. Douglas's alimony check is late. Furthermore, while I sympathize with your injury, it is no excuse for your repeated waste of this court's time with these frivolous and groundless motions. I don't want to see you in my courtroom again unless you have, not only a valid reason to ask for a reduction in spousal support, but the physical documentation to back up such a request. Your ex-wife's countersuit requesting you pay the attorney fees she incurred to fight this proceeding is hereby granted. Your motion for reduction in alimony is denied. Court is adjourned."

***

Brianna had to know how Rob lost his finger. It was one thing to say the neighbor's necklace showing up was a coincidence. It was entirely another to assume the gruesome finger presented by the crows wasn't Rob's.

Not one given to superstition, Brianna refused to believe that somehow the crows knew of her trouble with her ex-husband and decided to take matters into their own beaks. The whole notion that the crows she fed every morning could have possibly done something like this was ludicrous.

One of the few couples who Brianna was still on friendly terms with from her married life was Larry and Sue Conner. She called Sue on a fishing expedition to find out how Rob had come up one finger short. She prayed there was some reasonable explanation waiting at the other end of the phone line.

After the pleasantries were exchanged, Brianna did not even have to ask Sue what happened. Her friend brought it up first. She asked, "Bri, did you hear what happened to Rob?"

Acting like she had no idea what Sue was talking about, Brianna responded, "No, what?"

"It was really weird. He got his finger bitten off, if you can believe that."

"Really? How did that happen?" Brianna closed her eyes waiting for Sue's response.

"Larry said something about a flock of crows attacking him while he was asleep on a lounge chair by the pool."

Brianna bit her lip. "A murder," she muttered.

"Huh?" Sue asked.

"A group of crows is called a murder, not a flock." Sue said, "Okay, well, they murdered the ring finger on Rob's left hand." And then she giggled at her own joke.

Brianna was silent for so long, Sue asked, "Hello, Bri? Are you still there?"

"Crows, you say? How many were there?"

"I think Larry said three. Pretty crazy, huh? Maybe it was revenge of the birds. You always liked the feathered critters so much. Kind of ironic it was his wedding ring finger." Once again, Sue laughed.

When she realized Brianna wasn't laughing with her, she quickly added, "Sorry, guess that probably wasn't funny."

Brianna hurried off the phone. She dissolved into hysterical laughter that gradually turned to sobs. Once she finally had herself under control, she wiped her eyes, drank a cool draught of water and headed to the patio to have a never-imagined conversation with her crows.

Brianna looked at the Dogwood, one of the crows' favorite perches, and did not see them there. Nor were they on the fence or anywhere else visible in the yard. She peeked over the fence to make sure no one was in the neighbor's yard. This was one chat she would never want over-heard.

Brianna began cautiously, "Hey there, crows. You guys out here? We need to have a little talk, you and I." Then she dissolved into giggles again that threatened to turn right back into hysteria.

Brianna drew in a couple of deep breaths to quell the laughter bubbling up and trying desperately to overtake her. The situation was just so uncanny she couldn't even believe it was happening. She went inside and splashed cool water on her face. She drank a shot of bourbon then headed back outside.

"Okay, crows, now listen up, because I only plan on saying this once. If you lobbed off my ex-husband's finger, I am forbidding you from ever doing anything like that again...unless of course next time you want to bite off his...well never mind." That did it. Brianna came utterly unglued. She laughed so hard tears were streaming from her eyes and she couldn't catch her breath. She grew lightheaded and was forced to put her head between her knees to keep from passing out. It would take several minutes before she could regain her composure enough to continue this monologue. When she began speaking again, she heard a single caw in return. All at once the trio of crows landed in a line on the grass a few feet from where she sat.

Though her heartbeat sped up a little, she managed to keep the hysteria at bay this time. Having no prior experience calling off attack crows who were working on her behalf, the words did not come easily.

It was disconcerting looking at the three pair of black eyes trained intently on her face. Rising, Brianna said, "Hold that thought," and escaped back inside the house. She returned a moment later with the bottle of bourbon clutched in her hand.

Taking a long swig directly from the bottle, Brianna looked into each crow's eyes. She cautiously began again, "It seems like maybe you guys understand what I am saying when I talk to you. I still have a hard time believing you attacked Rob, but there certainly is evidence to support that theory. So that's why I am giving it to you straight here. For all I know all three of you are Rhode's Scholars and speak the Queen's English."

Brianna held up a hand, as though the bird's had just disagreed with her. She took another drink from the bottle of bourbon. "If that's true, please do me a favor and don't start talking now. I am freaked out enough without having to listen to you recite Shakespeare or something." In the middle of this monologue Brianna's phone rang. She looked down at the caller ID and groaned. It was Rob. Obviously furious with the judge for the beating he took in court today; he was calling to take his frustration out on Brianna again.

Under normal circumstances Brianna would have let it go to voicemail and then sicked Paula on him. But emboldened by the whiskey, she answered the call.

She got as far as listening to him thunder, "You ball breaking bitch!" before holding the phone away from her ear for the rest of his tirade.

Hearing Rob's voice roaring through the phone, the crows went crazy. They began agitatedly cawing and flying in circles around the yard. Startled by their violent reaction, Brianna jumped up from the table, knocking the bourbon bottle over and sending it crashing to the patio. Brianna watched in dismay as amber colored liquid ran in all directions. When she glanced back up, she was shocked to see all three crows had flown onto the patio and were diving directly at her.

Brianna uttered a startled squawk and dropped the phone. She ran into the house and slammed the back door behind her. As she looked through the glass, she watched in awe as the birds furiously attacked the phone. They began violently pecking at it, and scrambled to keep purchase with their claws. Brianna could not believe her eyes, as bits of plastic began flying from the phone trapped between them. Screeching loud and angry caws, they carried it off the patio. Both the phone and the crows disappeared into the foliage in a cloud of dust.

Shaken, Brianna cautiously opened the back door when the frenzy had passed. She stepped out onto the patio. If the crows showed any sign of aggression toward her she would flee right back indoors to safety. She didn't think she was in any danger, however. She realized it wasn't herself who their anger was directed at. It was Rob.

"Hey, guys. Where are you?" Brianna called toward the yard. The bushes shook and the largest of the three crows emerged. He voiced one soft caw and then flew up and out of the yard. A moment later his two companions followed suit and flew away.

Brianna knelt down and felt around underneath the bush where they had disappeared with the phone. Finding it, she assessed the damage. The case was splintered, with a zigzagging crack running right down the center. Though the screen was deeply gouged and covered in scratches, surprisingly, the phone was still operational. She dusted it off on her jeans and went back inside the house.

Rob called three more times. Brianna let the calls go to voicemail. She would call Paula in the morning and let her know the harassment had started up again. In the meantime, she had more important things to think about. Like what to do about the crows. She was starting to worry they might decide to attack Rob again.

The following morning when she went outside with the toast for them, there was a scatter of wildflowers in the place on her patio where the crows always left their gifts. She wondered if this wasn't their way of apologizing for yesterday's outburst. They were certainly remarkable birds. Frightening, but remarkable.

As she tossed the bread onto the lawn the crows flew into the yard and landed on the grass. They looked at Brianna before approaching the toast she had put out.

"Well, go on. Eat your breakfast. I'm not mad at you if that's what you are afraid of, but you have to leave Rob alone. As I recall from Sunday school, the bible says nothing about vengeance is mine sayeth the crows."

As they ate the bread the black birds did not spare Brianna another glance. Appearing completely uninterested in what she was saying, they finished the bread and flew off into the mild morning breeze.

Over the next few days everything seemed to return to normal. The morning routine continued, with the crows waiting for their breakfast and cawing good-naturedly. No gifts of dubious origin were left for Brianna on the patio. In fact, they left nothing for her at all. She hoped the crisis was over and the birds would not bother Rob again.

She could no longer convince herself that her crows were not responsible for maiming his hand. She understood that they had become fiercely loyal to her. What she could not figure out was how they knew where to find her ex-husband. These were no ordinary birds. While Brianna had never believed much in supernatural phenomenon, she recognized something of that nature was at work here. She couldn't afford the luxury of ignoring it anymore. However, there really was nothing she could do about the situation. It certainly appeared they were on her side. She didn't believe they would harm her. While she would remain vigilant to the crows behavior, she could not force them to stay away from Rob. All she could do was tell them to leave him alone and hope they would obey her request.

What was now of greater worry was Rob himself. His behavior since losing the fight to have Brianna's alimony cut had become increasingly violent and erratic.

Brianna didn't know what to worry about more; Rob harming her, or the crows harming him.

The escalation began with Paula calling Rob's lawyer and telling him to rein in his client. If the scathing phone messages continued, she told Silverstein she would file for another injunction. Rob ignored the warning and was levelled with another hefty fine.

That only made matters worse. The calls increased in volume and severity. In desperation, Brianna changed her phone number.

This so incensed Rob, he began nearly nightly visits to Brianna's house. In a drunken rage, he would bang on the front door, hurling offensive insults and calling her filthy names. He demanded she "stop robbing him blind."

Another restraining order was filed. It did nothing to dissuade him. Finally, out of his mind with fury from Brianna's refusal to open the door to his maniacal ravings, Rob stumbled to his car, shouting

threats over his shoulder. Intending to roar from the house with tires squealing, he slammed his Porsche into the wrong gear and floored it. Sailing over the curb into Bobby and Renee's front yard, he took out their mailbox and several flower beds, before plowing into their garage door and causing himself a mild concussion when the airbag deployed.

The police and paramedics were called. After spending three hours in the emergency room, Rob was charged with destruction of property, violating a restraining order and driving while under the influence. He spent two nights in county lock-up, until Ariel could arrange to make bail.

Brianna did not know if it was the head injury, or the time in jail and the battery of legal problems he was now facing, but something seemed to have done the trick. For two blissful weeks Rob left Brianna completely alone.

She gradually began to get her nerves back under control and stop bracing for the sound of his pummeling fists and vulgar obscenities booming outside her front door every night. Her neighbor's garage and the damage to their property was covered by Rob's insurance. Fortunately, they did not blame Brianna for her ex-husband's conduct.

She could not believe Rob had gone so completely crazy. While she always knew that money was his god, Brianna never dreamed he was capable of such out of control behavior. After all, he had a reputation to uphold as a respected surgeon. The court of public opinion always mattered so much to him in the past. She wondered if he knew he was putting his whole life in jeopardy by behaving so recklessly.

She didn't even want to think about what the crows were capable of if they got wind of Rob's misdeeds. Fortunately all of his dangerous pursuits had taken place late at night when they were in their nest asleep. Brianna realized she did not even know where the crows' nest was located. For all she knew they lived in one of the tall trees in her backyard. That thought caused a nasty shiver of fright to crawl up her spine. What if all the commotion had woken them, and they were even now planning retribution? She never dreamed life could become so insane.

A short time later, time would prove Brianna had no idea what true insanity really looked like. She found out not too long after convincing herself that both her ex-husband and the crows were done causing her any grief.

***

On an overcast Tuesday, Brianna awoke to a commotion out on her back patio in the early morning hours. Glancing at the clock next to her bed, she saw it was just after sunrise.

Having no idea what all the racket was, Brianna flung open the window shade in her bedroom. Taking in the unbelievable scene playing out below her in the backyard, she stumbled away from the window and screamed.

Literally hundreds of birds were whirling in a dizzying cloud on her lawn. They formed a tight sphere and appeared to be pecking and clawing at something caught between them. Brianna had never seen so many birds at once.

The way they were moving together in that frenzied dance was worse than anything from even Tippi Hedren's worst nightmare.

All were converging on an unknown victim, in a blinding array of colors, shapes and sizes. Brianna could not see where one bird ended and another began. Their claws were working, their beaks snapping, and God help whatever was caught in the middle of the murderous orb they had formed.

She ran from the bedroom, taking the stairs two at a time.

As she approached the back door she heard the mad cacophony of thousands of beating wings. Bartholomew hissed and charged between Brianna's feet and up the stairs, retreating to the safety of her bedroom.

Brianna cautiously opened the curtains on the back door. She watched in dumbstruck horror as the colorful shroud of madly pecking birds elevated into the sky. It was impossible to see if her trio of crows was a part of that insane roaring tapestry.

Brianna collapsed against the door as the thick veil of screaming feathers flew over the house and due south. Just as they were ascending over the trees, Brianna uttered an anguished moan.

Peeking from between all those madly rushing bodies was Rob's staring face. It was frozen in a death mask and covered in dozens of bleeding scratches. Where his right eye should have been was only a bloody gaping hole. She saw this grisly scene for only a few seconds before the birds disappeared over the horizon.

With shaking hands Brianna unlocked the back door and stepped out onto her patio. Apart from several brightly colored feathers lying on the patio and strewn about the yard, there remained no evidence of the unspeakable horror she had just witnessed.

She plucked a single sleek black feather from the Dogwood tree and staggered back onto the patio. Falling into a chair, she called weakly, "Hey, crows. Are you guys here?"

The morning remained eerily still, and silent as a tomb. Her feeder sat empty and there was nothing perched in any of the bushes or trees. For the first time since she moved in, there was not a single bird anywhere in Brianna Douglas's yard.

Eyes glazed over in shock; Brianna sat slumped against the table for several minutes. When the doorbell rang, she recoiled as though a canon had been fired next to her head.

Sucking in harsh gasps of air, she rose on wobbly legs and made her way to the front door. She did not recognize her visitors, but began shaking uncontrollably when she saw a police car parked in her driveway.

Convinced Rob's body had already been found, she was sure the men on her porch were there to arrest her. She was the only person alive with a motive to kill him. It would, of course, be futile to try and explain to the authorities what fate had actually befallen him. Who in their right mind would believe it? She barely believed it herself. Brianna hoped Paula knew a good criminal defense attorney.

Neither of the two men waiting at her front door wore a police uniform. They were in business suits. Brianna steeled herself for their accusations and opened the door.

They smiled politely and held up their badges for her inspection. "Mrs. Douglas?"

Unable to trust herself to speak, Brianna nodded.

"I am Detective Ramirez, and this is my partner Detective Soames. We are sorry to disturb you at this hour, but we have reason to believe your life may be in danger."

This was not what she was expecting to hear. For several seconds she did nothing but look back and forth between the two men, her brow knitted in confusion. Finally, Brianna whispered, "What?"

"Ma'am, we received a phone call this morning from a woman named Ariel Forbes. She claimed that her boyfriend — — your ex-husband, Robert Douglas, was on his way over to your house with a gun. According to Ms. Forbes, he was planning to kill you. We put out an APB on his vehicle and it was located about a block from here. We were afraid we might have been too late. Have you seen or heard from Mr. Douglas today?"

Brianna shook her head. Tears welled in her eyes and she sagged against the door frame. The detective who had done all the talking put a supportive arm around her waist.

He said sympathetically, "I know this is a lot to absorb. May we come in? We don't want to leave you alone until Mr. Douglas is apprehended. There are officers and a canine unit in the area looking for him. It's only a matter of time before we catch him."

Brianna allowed the officers inside. She looked nervously toward the backyard, but all was quiet there.

Brianna offered the detectives coffee, but her hands were shaking so badly she spilled the grounds all over the floor. Detective Soames wiped them up while Ramirez got the coffee pot going. Brianna excused herself to get dressed and went upstairs to her bedroom.

The full impact of what the detectives had told her hit her like a ton of bricks and she collapsed onto the bed. She now understood what this morning's hellish occurrence was all about. The birds had saved her life. Equally amazing; the skinny, anorexic bitch alerted the cops to Rob's plans in an effort to spare Brianna from his wrath. She supposed she should thank her.

***

Robert Douglas's body was never found. His disappearance was investigated and even made news headlines. The case was listed as unsolved in the police archives. His fate remained a mystery to everyone. Only Brianna knew the truth.

Eventually the birds returned to her yard——all except the crows. Brianna waited for them every morning and left toast for them on the grass, but they did not show up.

After several months, Brianna accepted that they probably weren't coming back. She missed them a great deal.

She reasoned they had been her guardian angels, and once they saved her from Rob, their job was done.

It was a pleasant surprise when the following summer she found a sparkling seashell waiting for her at the edge of the patio one morning.

She shaded her eyes against the sun and peered up into the Dogwood. The crows weren't there.

That was okay. She smiled and held up the shell anyway. "Thanks, this is very pretty. Come back and see me, okay? I miss you guys."

The next morning Brianna awoke to the familiar sound of the crows cawing, and looked out the window to see all three of them waiting patiently for their toast on the lawn.

The End.

CASE #95425

AS THE CROW FLIES

BY KRYSTAL LAWRENCE

Krystal Lawrence lives in the Pacific Northwest. She is the author of three novels, two vampire stories, Risen and Risen II: The Progeny, and a trilogy entitled, Be Careful What You Wish For. Her fourth book is due to be released this autumn and is entitled, Cat O'Nine Tales. Krystal's books are available through Amazon and all major book retailers. You can visit the author's website at www.darksidestories.com

CASE #: 42726

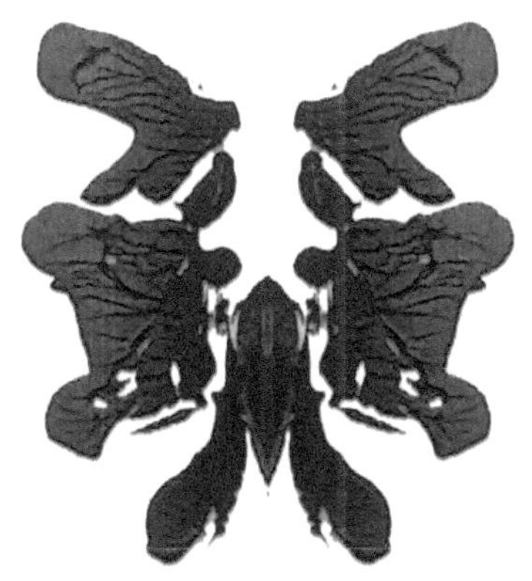

Even Odds by Virginia May

"Step inside girls," said the shabbily dressed man. "Zoltar knows all." A red glow flickered inside the tent.

"Let's go in," Maddie said, tugging on her older sister's arm.

"It's a waste of money. Everything here is a waste of money, rigged games, crummy rides, bad food, typical Scottish funfair," Elise complained. "Let's ride the Doom Coaster and go home."

A group of older kids walked by laughing and chatting. Distant screams of people on rides and carnival barkers coaxing customers reverberated around them. Rasping of metal on metal and the rumble of ride engines thrummed in the background, the smell of their exhaust not so strong here.

"Come on Elise, please? It's only 50p." Without waiting for an answer, Maddie slipped into the tent.

"Whatever." Elise followed.

Thick tent drapes closed behind the girls dulling the cacophony outside. The sound of Maddie's boots hitting the wooden floor echoed, making the space feel larger inside than it looked outside.

The fortune-telling machine loomed larger as they approached it. Letters above the window on the booth blinked: "Zoltar Speaks". The light cast eerie shadows around them. Behind the glass, Zoltar's black eyes stared out. His face, lit from below looked devilishly creepy.

Maddie dug a 50p coin from her backpack and dropped it in the slot. Music blared. They both jumped back. Zoltar's eyes lit up flashing fiery red. His head tilted back opening his mouth while his jaw stayed in place. A bell rang, a growl-like breath sounded. Words to the right of his head lit: "Aim ramp at Zoltar's mouth."

Maddie turned a handle on the front of the box moving the ramp. Zoltar's head rocked back and forth making the growling breathing noises each time his mouth opened. Another light on the front lit up:

"Zoltar says, ask your question."

"Are *all* the games here rigged?" Maddie asked, giggling. "Let's see if he answers that."

More creepy music played, bells rang. The words to the left of Zoltar's head lit: "Press red button to release coin."

Maddie pushed the button. Her coin rolled down the ramp and flew into Zoltar's mouth. Once more his head rocked, a final bell rang, and a card popped out of a slot below the window. The head settled into its original position and the lights went out leaving just the dim red glow and the blinking "Zoltar Speaks" sign.

Maddie read the card:

"Buy two tickets in the blackjack game, the money prize you will claim."

Elise rolled her eyes. "Nonsense! You saw the paper tickets on the ground. No odd numbers, you can't get twenty-one. They never pay out the money prize."

They left the tent when the man outside ushered more people through the entrance.

"But he answered my question. How did he know?" Maddie insisted.

"Honestly, Maddie! It wasn't a real person," Elise continued arguing as they headed for the blackjack game. "That answer fits a dozen questions. The cards are meant to get people to spend more money."

"I'm going to buy two tickets. It's only 40p and if you get twenty-one it pays £21."

"Whatever. It's your money," Elise said. "But after that, it's the Doom Coaster and we leave."

***

Maddie fiddled with the card turning it over and over as they waited in line at the blackjack game window. "Look! There's more writing on the card now!"

"Let me see," Elise said, yanking the card out of her sister's hand. "Think twice. Winners pay a price."

"Some kind of disappearing ink, just another trick," Elise said. "It's silly. Of course there's a price; the tickets aren't free."

Maddie hesitated then pushed her money through the ticket window to the burly man inside. He pushed two folded papers back, one pink and one blue. Carefully tearing the papers open, she saw two numbers that added up to twenty-one. Maddie squealed with joy.

A siren sounded and recorded clapping blared from a loud speaker along with an announcement that there was a winner. The man in the ticket booth traded the two tickets for £21 and congratulated the girls. "Fate is with you, choose wisely how you spend your prize," he said, holding the money tightly for a few seconds, making eye contact before letting go.

Walking to the coaster, the smells drifted from hot sugar to wet hay to cigarettes. Brightly colored clowns and acrobats passed on their way to the circus tent. A bored man dressed in brown and gray traded customers' money for balls to toss at milk

53

bottles no doubt too heavy to knock over. Music blared from loud speakers interrupted by an announcement the circus act would soon begin. The girls enjoyed the feelings, the sounds and smells, the excitement, their good fortune. Elise had changed her mind about all the games being fixed.

A man appearing from nowhere clutched Maddie's arm. "Buy me a bun? Please, I haven't eaten," he said.

She jerked her arm loose and the girls hurried away.

***

Standing in line for the coaster, Maddie saw new words on the card:

"Car 22 will take your breath, car 21 will cause your death,"

She handed the card to Elise. "I don't want to get on the coaster," Maddie said, trying to pull Elise out of the line.

"It's another trick. Don't be so gullible. I wanted to ride the coaster since we got here."

"Look!" Maddie pointed to the car in front as their turn came up to get in. "It's number twenty, that means the next car is number twenty-one!" She turned trying to leave but Elise held her arm.

"There is no car twenty-one, kid." A scruffy looking man held his hand out for their tickets. "All the cars have even numbers."

"Told ya. Now will you relax? That Zoltar thing's just a machine. Everything on that card is a coincidence, that's all."

The man pulled their seatbelts tight. "Keep yer hands and feet inside."

The wooden track clacked under the car as it climbed with jerking motions.

Maddie looked at the card still in her hand just as they crested the top:

"You didn't buy the man a bun, are you in car 22 or car 21?"

Both girls screamed in terror as the coaster car spilled over the top and sped down the track.

***

Carnival noises sounded distantly. Paper blackjack tickets, all with even numbers, littered the ground. Two sisters, one ten, one twelve, waited to be picked up by their father.

"I never want to come here again," the younger girl said.

"Told you it was fake," said Elise. "Made the Doom Coaster scarier. That was fun! Probably part of the trick all along."

The car they were waiting for pulled up. "Look!" Elise cried. "The plate on Dad's car! It has the number twenty-one on it!"

The End.

CASE #42726

EVEN ODDS
BY VIRGINIA MAY

56

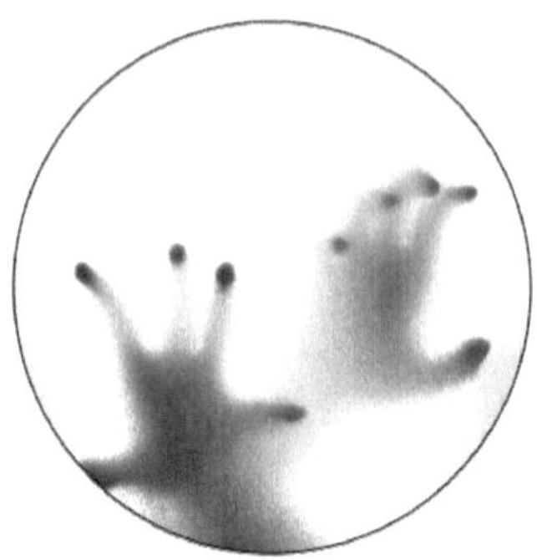

Virginia May writes Science Fiction, sometimes with a bit of the macabre. She's won several short story contests and has a near-finished novel. This is her second published short story. She lives in Washington State with her two dogs, on the edge between the forest in the backyard and the big city encroaching from the front.

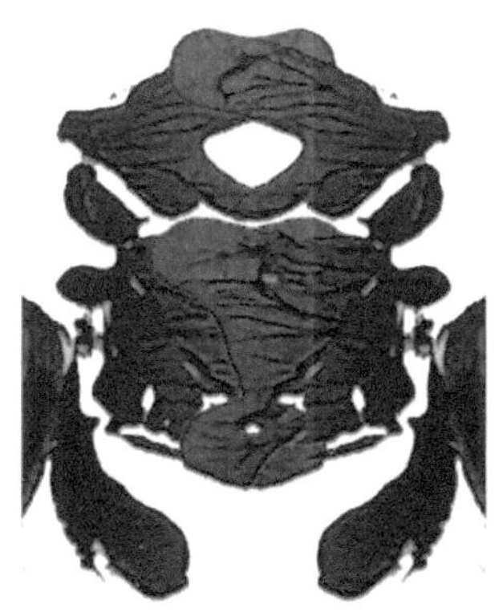

Lost And Found by Jennifer Canaveral

Sprinkles ran away again. She squeezed her skinny body through the wonky plank in the backyard fence and off she went. I saw the whole thing from the kitchen window and before I could reach the door, I heard her barking taper off as she ran down Gaunt Street. For an old Cocker Spaniel, she's got a lot of spunk left in her, more than an old man like me can handle. It's been nearly four days since she took off and I will not step away from this phone until someone finds her.

We were living in Shadow Brook the last time she ran off and the town was bigger than this one. I taped posters of Sprinkles on every lamppost in the neighborhood and it took just two days for someone to find her. It is amazing how fast things are found when a reward is thrown in, even just a measly hundred bucks. Joey, the young gentleman who found Sprinkles, said she was cold and shivering when he saw her pacing over a small pond about two miles away from our place. He picked her up the previous night but took it upon himself to bathe and feed her before calling me the next day. Joey. What a guy.

I was finishing up a new shed for the Randall family when Joey tried calling and he finally got ahold of me later that day. As if he hadn't done enough for my Sprinkles already, he wanted to drive her back to me, too. He said it would be no trouble at all. After all he had done, I told Joey I would save him the trip and pick up Sprinkles myself.

His house was on the outskirts of town and I was surprised to see the address led to a huge Victorian at the end of the road. The house seemed like it should be on a San Franciscan hilltop instead of a backcountry road but it was quite a sight. A luscious apple orchard decorated the backdrop of the exquisite mansion and for a moment, its beauty distracted me from everything else in my life, even my lost dog. I stepped out of my truck and stood there, admiring the view in silence.

"Lovely, isn't it?" a voice asked.

I turned to find a handsome young man in his twenties standing on the front porch of the house, smiling at me.

"Lovely? It's an absolute vision. I'm Albert Jeffries, Sprinkles owner." I said.

"Oh, wonderful. I'm Joey, as you might've guessed. A carpenter, eh?" Joey asked, pointing at my work belt.

"Yep, sure am. Just started doing odd jobs around town earlier this week. Is it just you in this big house?" I asked.

"Just me. Still looking for that special someone to make an honest man out of me." Joey said.

I walked towards the porch and we shook hands. His hair was slicked back and shined in the waning sunlight. He resembled a movie star, though no particular name popped in my head. Before I could figure it out, I heard Sprinkles bark and the thumping of her feet as she raced down the carpeted stairs inside Joey's home.

"Well, come on in, Mr. Jeffries. Sounds like Sprinkles has already sensed your arrival." Joey said.

We walked inside, where Sprinkles pawed at my legs until my creaky knees brought me down to her level. She leaped into my arms and drenched my face with slobbery kisses.

"I'm sorry but do you mind if I use your restroom?" I asked. "After you called, I jumped in my truck without a second thought. Not even the call of nature."

"Of course, Mr. Jeffries. It's just right over there under the staircase." "Thanks. Oh and hey, call me Al." "Will do, Al." Joey said.

I had to fight off Sprinkles to get the bathroom door closed but once I did, I took off my carpenter's belt and unzipped my coveralls, removing the sledgehammer I had strapped to my thigh. It was getting rusty on top and the handle felt strange in my hand. I was overdue for a new one but it was suitable for one more job. Just one more.

I opened the door to find Joey on his knees playing with Sprinkles, his back towards me. I tightened my grip on the sledgehammer and raised it high above my head. For a second, it looked as if I could deliver the blow without ever seeing his face but as I moved forward, my shadow crept over his body. He turned quickly and shot a terrified gaze into my eyes. Before he could utter a sound, I smashed the sledgehammer into his cheekbone, sending broken teeth and spurts of blood out of his mouth. Then I smashed his lower jaw. Then his other cheekbone. Finally, I drew a final blow down onto his skull and watched his body convulse on the hardwood floor like an epileptic off his anti-seizures. Sprinkles sat and observed daddy at work. My obedient, devoted companion.

I wiped the splatter off my face as I reached for my wallet inside my coveralls. I pulled out a crisp hundred-dollar bill and stuck it inside Joey's argyle sock then took his wallet from his slacks. Sprinkles and I left the house just before sunset with the apple trees gently swaying in the warm breeze behind us.

We left Shadow Brook later that evening, richer in pocket and spirit, and drove on for days. Before heading over to Joey's that day, I left the landlord first and last month's rent on the kitchen counter, to lull any red flags from flying. In my experience, missing tenants are only truly missed when their disappearance is accompanied by outstanding debts. I walked out of the apartment with a clear conscience and got in my truck without looking back. After about a week of driving, I stumbled upon the town of Everton and decided it was suitable for a temporary stay.

Sprinkles is out there somewhere, wandering around and looking pathetic for some unsuspecting sap to find. I printed a new set of posters and taped them on the local store windows and telephone posts, garnering plenty of sympathy from the locals. Of course, the phone number has changed. Pretty soon, I'll have to get a new truck and a new dog, too. The observant cop would find numerous Sprinkles disappearances a bit suspicious. The last thing a man needs is a cop with a hunch following him around and if there's a breadcrumb trail already laid out for him, the gig is up, baby.

It's too early to start searching for a new pup but I went ahead and bought a new sledgehammer from a hardware store about a hundred miles back. I burned the old one's handle for firewood and tossed the old head in a dumpster near Des Moines. This new head shines like a polished nickel, fresh out of the mint. The grip might take some getting used to but boy, am I eager to break this sucker in. I got a new hundred dollar bill ready for whoever finds Sprinkles and wherever they are, I can be there in a jiff to get that old doggie back home. All they have to do is give me a ring.

Sprinkles, oh Sprinkles, where can you be?

The End.

CASE #:70646

LOST AND FOUND

BY JENNIFER CANAVERAL

61

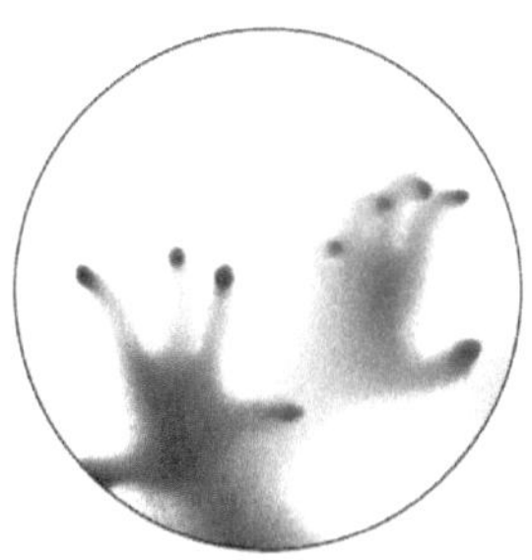

Details not released at this time

CASE #: 30900

Maintenance by Mike Payne

Upon awaking, he found himself in a cage. It'd been a boozy night, but he didn't remember…

He was chained to a table, everything but his head tied down.

The room housed several more cages, each with a captive inside.

His left forearm stung; a bandage dangled from it.

"Hello?"

"Quiet!" said someone in another cage.

"Where am I?"

"A clinic."

"What clinic?"

Footsteps. A pasty man in black appeared.

"You've heard of methadone clinics?" the pasty man said.

"Yeah-"

"You think only humans need to maintain their habits?"

He bent down and grinned. His teeth were speckled with red stains.

The End.

CASE #30900

MAINTENANCE
BY MIKE PAYNE

Mike Payne is a writer and former comedian whose credits include Pseudopod.org and The Flash Fiction Press. On Twitter: @ greatmikepayne.

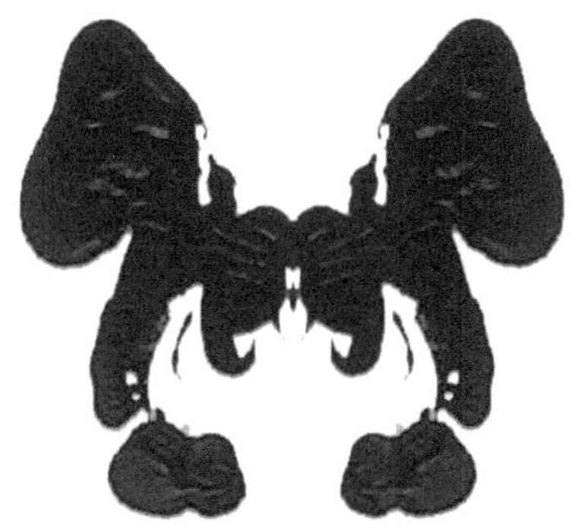

The Handshake by Cindy O'Quinn

Shoot for the moon because you'll never hit the stars.

This was my brother's advice when I told him I wanted to be a writer. Good ole Dell Eastlin knew what he was talking about from time to time. Dell was five years my senior and I have always looked to him for advice on everything from – what clothes make me look the coolest, to – how do I go about getting a date with the popular girl, to – should I drive three hours to try and meet my favorite author? That last one would prove to cause me a great deal of trouble. But would I go back and do things different if I could? Maybe. Probably not.

I am Torrence Eastlin, the writer. Some of you may have heard of me. I was only fifteen when I let my brother in on my goal to become a successful writer. When I was twenty and in my second year of college I heard from my creative writing teacher that Hudson Greenbrier was going to be at a bookstore in Sweet Wine, Virginia, the following weekend. This was of great interest to me because Hudson Greenbrier was my all-time favorite writer. He was right up there in the same ballpark as Stephen King, in my opinion. Sweet Wine was a three hour drive from Charlottesville and who's to say if my teacher knew what she was talking about? No one else I talked to had heard any news of Hudson Greenbrier coming to Virginia. Nevertheless, I asked big brother if I should take a chance and make the six hour round trip to Sweet Wine. He told me to go for it and that's just what I did.

There was magic in the air on that Saturday. If you believe in that sort of thing. I never did until that day. It was October twenty-fourth. That's peak time for fall foliage in my part of Virginia. As I drove east on I-64 it looked as though the trees were exploding with extreme colors like the fireworks at Crozet Park had on the fourth of July. The reds and oranges were brighter than I had ever seen and the pops of red stood out like Red Hots sprinkled on the white icing of my birthday cake when I turned twelve. I was a big Red Hots fan back then.

I had been so distracted by the extraordinary leaves that I almost missed my exit. I rolled into the small town of Sweet Wine at half past eleven and could have rolled out a minute later because it was that small of a town. Turns out that Sweet Wine was one of those hole in the wall places that you would miss if you blinked for more than a millisecond. There was a gas station, bank, grocery mart, and a bookstore. The latter was the only store that I was concerned about. The sign painted on the window read STONE SOUP BOOK SHOP. There was no flyer in the window telling about the famous Hudson Greenbrier making an appearance. My heart started to droop at the idea that the trip had been for nothing. Telling myself I had the beautiful fall foliage to look forward to on the drive back did little to lift my spirit. I hardly noticed when one of those supermini cars pulled up to the curb. It was a white *Geo Metro,* nothing special. But I soon took notice when the man driving the car stepped out. It was more like he folded himself out of the tiny contraption and then unfolded once he was free of it. He was very tall. Had to be 6'5" at least.

Hudson Greenbrier is tall, I told myself. I could feel myself losing color and my heart that had been drooping moments earlier now started tap-dancing in my chest. This must be how it feels for a music lover to meet Eric Clapton. I'm a word lover and Hudson Greenbrier was less than five feet away from me. I felt so silly to be getting worked up like a teenage girl but this was my idol. I wanted to be like this man. I wanted to pick his brain. I wanted to be as good a writer as him. No. Half as good would be just fine by me. And there I stood trembling like a Chihuahua on crack. I watched the tall writer as he stretched and twisted from side to side. He was probably trying to work the kinks out after being squished up in that match box of a car. It reminded me of the snake in a can I bought from the gag store one time. It was a twelve-inch springy snake stuffed in a four-inch fake peanut can. I got Dell real good with it.

The writer walked around his car and towards me. He was coming my way. All I could think was, *What do I say?* And then it happened. I said, "Hello, Mr. Greenbrier. I love your words." It's official. I'm a fucktard.

He smiled at me and said, "Thanks. I hope you enjoy my stories as well." Then Hudson Greenbrier went inside Stone Soup Book Shop and my opportunity to pick his brain was gone forever because he would never take me seriously after that.

I started to walk away and then went back. I did this three times before finally getting the nerve up to go into the bookstore. A couple of dozen folding chairs had been set up near the back of the store. They were facing a small podium. Several people had gone inside while I was in the midst of pacing back and forth outside and they were now sitting in the front row of chairs. All for the best I thought. I surely wouldn't want to be in the front now that he knows I'm an idiot, so I took a chair nearer the back and off to the side. I looked down at my trembling hands and realized they were empty. I hadn't brought one of the writer's novels for him to sign. Frantic by this point, I looked around and saw a collection of Hudson Greenbrier's books on display. I made a mad dash and grabbed the first one I could get my hands on and then took it to the clerk. She asked, "This is a first edition. Are you sure this is the one you want?"

I could feel my face bloom with a rush of heat. "Oh. No, I have that first edition. I'll get a different novel." Of course, I didn't already have a first edition copy nor did I have the two hundred bucks to buy this one. I went back to the stack and picked one of his more recent novels. Of course, I did already have a copy of this one at home. In fact, I had all of his books. I could feel that my face was still flaming as I returned to my seat.

It was noon when Hudson Greenbrier stepped up to the small podium and began talking. And for the two hours that followed he taught me everything I thought I would ever need to know about writing. There were other people there, the chairs had filled up quickly and there was only standing room beyond that. But like I told you before, it seemed a magical day and for two hours it was just me and my favorite author. I was in a tunnel of sorts and the bright light ahead shone on Hudson Greenbrier, all six foot five of him. The writer's hair, that had once been a rich auburn color, was now only a cotton tuft, but the brain not far below it was all accounted for and still at the top of his game. Once the talking had ceased, my tunnel opened back up to the room that was the Stone Soup Book Shop. He glanced my way and I realized those gray eyes had not actually been focused on me for the previous two hours, and that was okay.

Everyone stood, that wasn't already standing, and gave the writer a standing O that lasted at least five minutes. When it was over we formed a makeshift line that led right up front and center to the little podium. The clerk came and moved the podium against the wall and motioned the writer to a chair with cushions behind a small table and there was one of the folding chairs in front of the table. Well, I thought, maybe I'll get the chance to redeem myself after the tomfuckery I pulled in front of the bookstore earlier.

The writer was the perfect gentleman as fans oohed and aahed all over him. He patiently posed for pictures even when the nonagenarians lollygagged and held up the flow of the line. He not only autographed his novels but also obliged one fan by signing his forearm. The fan was then headed to the nearest tattoo parlor to have Hudson Geenbrier's name forever inked on his skin.

My turn eventually came. I rubbed the palms of my sweaty hands on my jeans while I went over and over in my head what I would say to my hero. I stepped forward. Of course, I did the same goofy things as everyone else had before me. I took a selfie with the writer and then sat down on the metal chair across the table from him. I hadn't laid the novel down and I had yet to say a word. Hudson Greenbrier's distinct deep voice broke the silence. "Would you like for me to sign that book?"

I looked down, horrified that I still had the book clutched against my chest, and said, "Oh shit! I'm sorry. You must think I'm a real ignoramus." I slid the book across the table.

The writer smiled and said, "Trust me, you are holding it together just fine. For starters you haven't asked me to sign any part of your body and you are not crying."

"It's just that you are it for me. You are my all-time favorite writer. I have everything you have ever published. When I pictured meeting you, I never thought I would fall to pieces like some freaky number one fan," I said, trying to pull my shit together.

"Well, let's try again. Is there something you would like to ask me? Please don't ask where all of my ideas come from because I can't make up one more story for that question. The ideas just come and that's the only way I can explain it." The writer said.

I asked, "Do you ever get annoyed when people always refer to you as *The Whodunnit Writer?* There's so much more that you write besides murder mysteries, which are great. I know for me anyway, your nonfiction novel *All About Me – The Writer* is my favorite. I loved the stories you told about growing up and getting started in writing. And then there's your fantasy series, it's terrific."

Hudson Greenbrier leaned forward and paused a sec before answering. "I'll tell you something about writing, son. It makes no difference to me at all what tag the world clips by my name. All that matters is that the readers enjoy my work. As long as that happens, I'll keep at it."

"Yeah, I guess I never thought of it that way. Thanks for sharing that with me. I just hope I can have half of your talent someday," I said. Smiling as I realized he had called me son. My day could not get any better. Or could it?

The writer quickly added, "Don't sell yourself short. Aim high not low."

I glanced back at the line of fans and realized I had hogged far more time than I should have. I stood and reached out my hand to my favorite writer. His enormous hand clasped down around mine causing it to all but disappear. That's when, once again, I felt that magical haze that had been hovering close all day. I was back in that tunnel just like before when the writer had been speaking at the podium. This time there was actually a white glow around the two of us. Our hands together produced an electrical heat that I could feel up my arm and into the base of my skull. It felt like it lasted an hour, when in all actuality it had probably only been a matter of several seconds. When the tunnel and light melted away, the writer was handing me the novel he had so graciously autographed for me, and saying, "Good luck with your writing."

"Okay. Thank you." I said. Before walking away I saw something in Hudson Greenbrier's eyes that hadn't been there before. Fear.

The drive back to Charlottesville was nothing like the drive to Sweet Wine. My mind was in a fog and I was unaware of my surroundings. The fall foliage could have turned black and I wouldn't have noticed. I wasn't fully alert again until I pulled into the driveway at home. I looked down in the passenger seat and saw Hudson Greenbrier's book. I picked it up and looked inside. I hadn't even bothered to look at what the author had written. It read:

Here's to Torrence Eastlin, the next big deal. I know there will be many who love your words.

Hudson Greenbrier

I read the words over and over. I couldn't remember, for the life of me, having told him my name. I must have though. In my star-struck state I must have told him my name. How else would he have known? There was a peck on my window that caused me to slam the book shut like I was hiding a secret. It was my brother and he was laughing at having caused me a fright. Dell asked, "Well, did you meet him?"

I answered as I got out of the car. "Hell yes I met him. Here's the selfie to prove it." I handed my cell over to my brother. "He signed his book for me and then we talked a while." I went on to tell my brother how I had made an ass out of myself outside the bookstore. He got a real kick out that. I didn't tell him about the tunnel, the light, or the fact that I didn't recall having given the writer my name.

Later that night in my room when the day had finally started to calm down I wrote a three thousand word short story. I thought it was the best I had ever written and I wasn't the only one to think it was good. My parents and my brother all agreed that I should submit it to *Word Burner Magazine* so I did. A day later I received an email saying they wanted to publish my story in their next issue. I received three hundred dollars for that short story. I went on to write seven more short stories and they all sold. With each story published, my paycheck grew by another hundred dollars. Each time I sat down and started writing I could feel myself floating back into that tunnel I was in the day I had met Hudson Greenbrier. Never once did I question it, I just chalked it up to having been inspired by my favorite writer. As I look back, deep down I knew it was much more than inspiration. It went on this way for three months until I decided it was time to move on from short stories and on to writing my first novel.

Within a month I had written a three-hundred-page murder/mystery fiction novel and had gone back over it twice to weed out any mistakes, which there were very few. My contact at *Word Burner Magazine* referred me to the editor at *Nelson County Books*, a small publishing house, in nearby Afton, Virginia.

I met the editor, Tut Harper, a week later. In Virginia he was known as *The King of Editors*. Hence the nickname, Tut. I'll never forget that first meeting. It had been frigid all of January and now into February the mercury refused to rise. I walked into the building, which was actually an old converted train caboose. Funny enough, the caboose looked right at home sitting in a valley between two rather large mountains. Tut Harper stood up from behind his desk, a slab of varnished petrified wood on top of two wine barrels. There was a vineyard close by. He was definitely not what I imagined when I pictured an editor, especially one known as *The King of Editors*. He looked to be in his early fifties with a beard that put me in the mind of two members of the band, ZZ Top. Dressed in thread-bare Levis and a flannel shirt. I thought for a minute I was in a paper towel commercial.

Before I could say anything, because I was busy taking it all in, he spoke up. "You must be Torrence Eastlin, the next big deal."

Did he really just say that? That's what Hudson Greenbrier had written in my copy of his novel. Part of what he had written anyway. I knew I hadn't shared that detail with anyone at *Word Burner Magazine*. So why had he said that of all things? I tried to hide my confusion as I reached out to shake the editor's hand and confirmed, "I'm Torrence Eastlin alright but I don't know about being the next big deal."

Tut continued, "Oh I am sure of it. Kid, I've got to hand it to you.

I haven't seen writing this good since I was a kid and reading my first Hudson Greenbrier novel."

My skin felt hot from the sudden rush of blood flowing to my upper half. Could my writing really be compared to my idol,

Hudson Greenbrier? I never stopped to consider if my style was similar to his. Why would I? He was up there in that, out of my reach writing field. *Shoot for the moon because you'll never hit the stars,* is what Dell had advised me when I told him I wanted to be a writer. Hudson Greenbrier was the star and Tut Harper was comparing my first novel to that very same star. That fall day in October started replaying in my mind. It had been a magical day. My heart catapulted into a series of flips like cartwheels and round-ups. I could see me on that magical day as I reached out to shake the author's hand. His massive hand had swallowed mine much the same way a large mouth bass swallows a Crazy Leg Jig and I had felt something in that handshake. Even back then I had tried to convince myself it had only been the excitement of meeting my favorite writer. When our hands gripped, I had felt a trickle of electricity that reminded me of the stray voltage that surrounds an electric fence when it does not have a ground rod in place. That trickle had turned into a full jolt as it traveled up my arm and into the base of my skull. It was as though the energy had been seeking for something. My brain.

Tut Harper was staring at me like I was the main attraction at a local freak show when he spoke again. "Torrence, are you alright? I didn't mean to worry you or anything. It's not like I was accusing you of plagiarism. Unless, of course, you have discovered a treasure trove of Greenbrier's unpublished works."

"Oh, no." I stuttered and then felt like I needed to say more. "I did meet him though. A few months back I listened to him speak over in Sweet Wine. Afterwards there was a meet and greet and he signed one of his novels for me. It kind of took me by surprise when you referred to me as 'the next big deal' because Greenbrier wrote that in the book he signed."

"Hell yeah say." Tut stated.

"Really he did. No shit." I assured the editor. Tut Harper laughed and said, "I believe you."

I continued, "He is my favorite writer and it would be a dream come true if someone thought my writing was half as good as his. But I don't want anyone to think I copied him in any way."

The editor ran his hand down his long beard for a moment then said, "I think it's only natural for writers to emulate the style of their most liked authors. As far as you copying him goes, well, I know you haven't done that because I am pretty sure I have read all of his work. It is the way your words flow that resonates as being similar to Hudson Greenbrier's work. Trust me kid, all writers want their words to flow as well as his. You have nailed it with your first novel. You are going to sell a lot of books."

I signed with *Nelson County Books* that very day and on the fourth of July weekend my novel, *The Hot Pistol,* was released. Even though the book was well received I continued to have some reservations. By Labor Day, *The Hot Pistol* had landed on that coveted list of best sellers in New York. It was the following month when Trena Foxcroft, dedicated assistant to Hudson Greenbrier, called me. She told me that Mr. Greenbrier requested a meeting with me. I knew it. It had all been too good to be true. What could I do? I agreed to the meeting.

The dreaded meeting was set for October 24th. The date definitely started the bells to ringing but it was not until the day of that it dawned on me that October 24th was the same day that I had driven to Sweet Wine and met my favorite author one year ago. Was it merely a coincidence? I thought not. Something else that was not a coincidence was the fact that a novel had not been released by Hudson Greenbrier this year and he had released a book every summer like clockwork for decades. Had his writing talent actually been transferred to me with that handshake?

I awoke early on the morning of the twenty-fourth in a cold sweat just as I had each morning since agreeing to the meeting. My nights had been filled with nightmares and they all had the same theme; Hudson Greenbrier ripping the flesh from my right hand and devouring it. The days were not much better. I questioned every sentence I wrote and wondered if I had read it somewhere before. Nothing I wrote felt like it belonged to me.

My drive to meet my favorite author would not take as long this time. I was to meet him in Vesuvius, which was less than an hour away. Hudson Greenbrier had leased a small farmhouse from fellow author, Van Stevens, for a couple of months. I was familiar with Mr. Stevens' work and I considered him an excellent horror writer who could scare the living shit out of a person. But in the end, we all have our favorite and Hudson was mine. As I drove along on Rt. 11 I noticed for the first time this fall that the leaves were devoid of all their brilliant colors. The trees only appeared to be carrying different shades of brown this season. I searched the sky for any signs of the sun but was met by ominous gray clouds that hung heavily over every mountain that surrounded me. A feeling of suffocation forced me to roll down my window. The air that slapped against my face felt hateful and too cold for a typical fall day. But today was proving to be far from typical. Decaying leaves swept across the road and I could almost hear them whisper warnings. I had no doubt that this day had been tainted with the opposite of magic. One year ago I had somehow received something via a magically lit tunnel that had vibrated with energy and it had been good. Maybe it had come to me by mistake and today its rightful owner would take it back. Or try.

I pulled in front of the little farmhouse in Vesuvius at half past eleven which was precisely the same time I arrived at the bookstore one year ago. Hudson Greenbrier's little white *Geo Metro* was in the driveway. It was parked behind a car with a cover on it. I could see red paint peeking out from under the tarp and knew right away it was Van Stevens' little red *Corvair* which had been mentioned in his novel, *Classic*. Hudson Greenbrier opened the door before I had the chance to knock. I quickly slipped my hands deep into my jean pockets in an effort to avoid shaking hands with the author. I hoped it wasn't obvious but I had no intention of giving back my new skills as a writer that easily. The author glanced down at my arms and then stepped aside and gestured with his large ghost-like hand for me to come inside. A gesture that felt ominous. The way the door snapped shut reminded me of a guillotine slamming down on its intended victim. I sensed that the author could tell I was anxious. I was sure I saw the slightest trace of a smile on his face which he tried unsuccessfully to hide. The two of us stood there in the hall, me with my hands tucked in my pockets, and Hudson with his ghostly white arms crossed at his chest, just staring at each other. Who would make the first move, the seasoned writer or the newbie? He had invited me here so I decided to wait him out.

The quiet of the farmhouse shattered when Hudson's commanding voice broke into my thoughts. "My assistant, Trena Foxcroft, has gone into town to pick up some lunch for us. She told me that you seemed hesitant about meeting with me. If I remember correctly, and I'm sure I do, you were so eager to talk when we last met. Has there been a change of heart? Perhaps I am no longer your favorite author, as you declared when I autographed a book for you."

Every word in the English language seemed to briefly slip from my mind. Eventually I answered, "Of course you are still my favorite writer. I guess I am just feeling a little off today. Maybe if you told me what this meeting was about it would help."

Hudson Greenbrier had a puzzled look on his face as he said, "I assumed Trena had told already told you why I requested this meeting." He continued, "Did you know that Van Stevens had hit a rough patch for about a year? He had some serious problems with his eyes and just about went blind. Things turned around for him though while he was staying here at this little farm. Van got the help he needed for his vision, as well as, motivation with the novel he was working on. Van and I have been friends for decades so when I asked if I could stay here for a while he didn't hesitate to say yes."

Cautiously I asked, "Are you going through a rough patch? I couldn't help but to notice that you have not released a book this year." "No, I'm not going through a rough patch. The story I'm currently working is a trilogy and I prefer to complete it before releasing the first book." Hudson seemed to be studying my face as he talked.

I didn't hear a car pull up so I had quite the start when the front door banged shut and Trena walked into the living room.

She was carrying two large bags with what I assumed to be the lunch Hudson had mentioned earlier. I stood and took the bags from her. She smiled and led me to the kitchen. For whatever reason, I was in no hurry to return to the conversation I was having with Hudson Greenbrier. Did I still believe I had received magical writing abilities through his handshake and he invited me here today to take back what was rightfully his? I had not noticed that Trena Foxcroft had stopped unpacking the bags and was now staring at me.

Trena cleared her throat and my eyes shot up and discovered her pale green eyes looking into mine. "Your novel, *The Hot Pistol*, is climbing the charts quickly. It's no wonder."

Suddenly I felt like I was twelve and had never spoken to someone of the opposite sex. "Does that mean you have read it?"

"Yes I read it and liked it very much. You are a talented writer." She looked away for a moment. I was certain that I saw a look of sadness on her face. Trena continued, "Go back in and I will let you two know when I have lunch set up."

I did as told but I could not shake the feeling that the woman felt bad for me for some reason. Maybe she knew Hudson was about to take back what was his all along.

Hudson looked up at me and said, "Son, you look as though you have the weight of the world on your shoulders."

Fuck it. I'll just throw caution to the wind and get it over with. "Hudson, something happened one year ago when we shook hands. Something magical. I felt it and if you say you didn't then you are lying. Did you invite me here today to take it back?"

The writer had a creepy Chesire cat's grin on his face which made him look like the fucking crypt-keeper. "Son, I'm afraid I don't know what you mean. If it's a sexual thing I must be upfront and tell you I am not gay. I'm flattered but I can't say I had a magical moment with you so there's nothing to take back." The smile faded but the big yellow horse-like teeth still showed.

He's fucking lying. I never noticed just how creepy this man really was, not until now anyway. Now what? If I don't say something, he will think I'm off my rocker.

Hudson offered, "Perhaps when we first met you became overwhelmed at the idea of meeting someone that you regarded so highly. And now things are a little more relaxed and you are disappointed to discover I am just a regular Jo. That can happen when you put someone up on a pedestal. No one can measure up to such high expectations."

Everything he was saying made perfectly good sense. Could I have really been so stupid? Magic? I shook my head and said, "Hudson, I'm sorry. You must be right. I've been having crazy thoughts that somehow your gift for writing had accidently been transferred to me in that handshake and you only invited me here to take it back. Pretty fucked up huh?"

Hudson's laugh was but a murmur. "I'll have to say you have quite the writer's imagination. It would make for a good story, that's for sure."

From the kitchen Trena called us in for lunch.

There were two places set at the small kitchen table. I felt disappointed that Trena would not be joining us. As if reading my thoughts Hudson insisted his assistant join us for lunch. She did so without argument. The meal had come from The Blue Sky Café and consisted of vegetable soup and smoked turkey sandwiched with avocado. Trena had made fresh squeezed lemonade.

My stomach rumbled as I took the first bite. I had been too anxious for breakfast and my stomach was now letting me know it. The soup and sandwich were great but the lemonade wasn't hitting on much. After just one sip I found it to be a little too bitter for my tastes. I didn't want to offend Trena and was glad when Hudson added sugar to his own glass then passed the sugar bowl to me. Three heaping spoons of sugar later the bitterness was gone. Almost.

Towards the end of the meal Hudson excused himself stating his aged bladder wasn't what it used to be which I found to be a hilarious thing to say. I should have felt a bit of guilt by my outburst of laughter, but I did not. Once the writer was out of the room Trena picked up my half empty glass of lemonade. I proceeded to protest and she shushed me with her finger.

She moved close to my ear and whispered, "You were half right with your suspicions. Something did happen when you shook hands with Hudson, although it's not what you had suspected. He didn't give you any special writing ability. You already had it. I'm sure you have heard people say, *I smell talent.* Well, Hudson Greenbrier can do that. He can literally smell talent and once he has your scent, he is relentless like a Komodo dragon. He will be back soon and he will take away your talent. Torrence, you are good and I don't want this to happen to you. Do you understand what I'm saying?"

I was floating on a magic carpet and Trena Foxcroft was putting a damper on my ride. Had I heard her correctly? Hudson Greenbrier was going to come back and take away my ability to write. The bitter taste was back in my mouth again. I needed something to drink. Not lemonade. The lemonade was tainted. "Bitter taste." I mumbled.

Trena nodded her head yes. "There was Librium in the lemonade. You didn't get the full dose. Do you hear me? Snap out of it before it's too late!" Trena went to the counter and poured me a fresh lemonade. Before coming back to the table she emptied and washed the original glass and put it in the drainer. "Here drink this." She pushed the glass up to my mouth and I drank.

"I won't shake his hand." My words slurred.

Trena explained further, "I wish it was that simple, regretfully it's not. The handshake only confirmed your writing talent. What he will do to you to take your gift away will all but kill you. Hudson Greenbrier is a monster." The assistant abruptly stopped talking and cocked her head to the side. The gesture made her look like a cocker spaniel that just heard something of utmost interest. After several seconds of intense concentration, she returned her focus to me. "He will drain you as though he's a human leach and then toss you aside like a cheap deflated balloon. Anything you ever imagined as a terrified child late at night will not compare to Hudson Greenbrier." Trena shook her head as though trying to erase the image from her scarred mind.

The magic carpet I was floating on suddenly started to tear and I could feel myself falling. The quickness of the fall lifted my stomach and caused it to lurch dangerously close to my throat bringing the bitter taste back to my mouth. I could feel myself turning bottle green inside and out as I started gagging. Trena shoved my almost empty soup bowl up under my chin as bitter veggie pieces filled my mouth. Vomit splashed from the bowel and over the assistant's hands. I cringed at the sight and then vomited once more. With the bitter drug mostly out of me I felt considerably better. As calmly as I could I asked, "How can I stop him?"

The assistant rung her hands as she answered, "I would tell you to just get in your car and drive like a bat out of hell but it would do little good. He has your sent now and you have what he needs. I'm afraid you will have to fight to keep what is yours."

Now I was the one shaking their head. "Are you fucking serious? This is too much. It can't be real. If you knew he was a monster then how could you continue working for him?" I struggled to get to my feet and then staggered as I tried to remain standing.

Trena Foxcroft looked rather ill as she considered my questions. "I was once in your position. I too was a gifted writer, but before I could publish my first work Hudson discovered me. I had nowhere to go after he took it all away. I was lost without my words. He offered to take me in and I accepted. It was as close as I was ever going to get to writing and I needed to at least be near it. I know you can't understand that, but that it's how I felt."

I was beginning to understand. Writing had been everything to Trena just as it is everything to me. She could not stand the thoughts of another person losing such a gift. "I'm sorry Trena. It is brave of you to try and help me." There were footsteps coming from the hall. A look of sheer terror blanketed Trena's face. She still had the bowl of soup puke in her hands when Hudson Greenbrier walked into the room.

He looked at us standing there and grimaced. The expression wrinkled his thin skin into ugly folds that hung below his sharp jawline. "You can't leave yet Torrence. You haven't even finished your soup." He looked at his assistant and the bowl clinched in her hands. "Put that back down Trena. Our guest hasn't finished with it."

Both Trena and I tried to protest, but Hudson would have no part in it. Trena sat the bowl back down on the table in front of me. I could see the panic in her eyes. I held onto the table as I eased myself back down in the chair. Trena returned to her seat as well. Hudson Greenbrier's eyes darted back and forth between the two of us.

He insisted, "Go ahead now. That soup is far too tasty to waste." I looked into Hudson's face and saw a look of enjoyment. Was he aware of what had taken place during his absence? I couldn't take the chance so I picked up the spoon and dipped it into the bowl. My only hope was that the soup and puke had not completely mixed together. I lifted the spoon to my lips and there it hung in midair for a second. It took all my will to open my mouth, but I did it. I put the spoon in and tilted it so the mixture would fall into my mouth and I swallowed without chewing or even breathing for that matter. My stomach churned and lurched and I gagged. I reached for the glass of lemonade and in the process knocked the soup bowel over dumping the remaining contents. Was it on purpose? Definitely. What was Hudson going to do? Surely he wouldn't have Trena to scrape it from the tablecloth and put it back in my bowel.

Hudson Greenbrier pushed away from the table and said, "Well then, it looks like lunch is over. Shall we return to the living room?"

I needed to know if any of this madness was real or not so I said, "No. I need to get back home now. I hadn't planned on staying this long." Hudson smiled his biggest yellow horse bucked teeth smile yet and replied, "Oh I don't think that is going to happen. Not yet anyway.

We have some unfinished business to take care of first. I get the feeling that my assistant has filled you in on my plans. Am I correct?"

I was as honest as I dared to be. "Trena only told me that you were interested in my talent. She told me nothing more." The palms of my hands were wet with sweat. My head felt as though I was at the top of a double Ferris wheel and the seat I was locked into was rocking back and forth far too hard. "I would be willing to set up another meeting with you. For the time being though, I really should be getting on the road."

"Perhaps I didn't make myself clear before so I will do so now. You will not leave from here until I say you can go."

And with that Hudson placed one of his oversized hands on my shoulder and squeezed so hard that I thought my flesh would tear from the bone. I tried to jerk away from his grip. When that failed I cried out, "Let go of me!" And he did. I rubbed the skin on my shoulder which continued to scream from pain. I gripped the arms of the chair and pushed myself up. The room seemed to tilt momentarily but leveled out. My chair was the only thing separating me from Hudson. I put one hand on the back of the chair and pushed it towards the man as I started for the door. This effort only slowed him by a second or two before he was on me. It all seemed too bizarre to be real. Surely I could take this elderly man if I had to. I drew back my fist, hesitating only for a second before throwing the punch. I braced myself for what would surely be the sound of his big yellow horse teeth breaking in his mouth. I was wrong. The noise I heard was coming from me. It was the sound of my own screams that filled my head.

My fist had made contact but it had engaged an open and waiting mouth. Hudson's mouth had suddenly opened like a trap door and a gaping hole exposed a circle of razor sharp teeth that had been hidden behind the large yellow bucked teeth. In the center of the multiple rows of little razor teeth was a sucking organ not unlike that of an elephant's trunk. The suction cup pulsed like a beating heart. I tore my eyes away long enough to look down at my hand which was still balled into a fist. The razor teeth had sliced through the skin on my knuckles exposing bone.

Flesh hung in dripping ringlets from my hand. I tried to open my hand and it took on the appearance of a poor version of the moles hiding underground in that game where you whack the animal on its head to make them go down. Only the moles were my knuckles and the ground was my torn skin. Call me a sissy if you want, but everything went black after that. In some far off place I could hear voices.

"You must not have given him enough of the Librium." Hudson Greenbrier was accusing his assistant.

Trena screamed at her boss, "You can't do this anymore! I won't let you!"

Hudson laughed at the woman, "And who is going to stop me? Surely not you. I had pity on you once. I am certain that it will not happen a second time. So if you want me to continue allowing you to exist in even my giant literary shadow you better do as you are told. We have a good thing going here so don't fuck it up."

Tears welled up in Trena's angry eyes. "You are wrong. This is not a good thing. You steal talent from gifted writers. You suck their reason for living right out of them like a vampire. Only you are worse because the venom that you leave behind corrodes within their bloodstream making them weak and feeble until they wither away and die the way the others did from your past." This statement created gooseflesh to rise on Trena's arms because she was one from his past, yet she was still holding on to life.

This angered the boss. "It was not my choice to be this way. If my father hadn't moved us to Lake Ontario I would have never been in that water infested with the lamprey. I survived the attack as well as overcoming the infection that followed. Can I be to blame for reaping the benefits of a terrible tragedy? What would you have had me do? Maybe follow in the footsteps of fisherman father. We both know that would have been no life for me. I deserved better after what I had gone through."

The assistant now pleaded, "You have had a good run. It's time for you to stop hurting people and let life run its course. Torrence Eastlin is a one of a kind writer and he has the right to experience being at the top. You have had far more than your share."

That's it. I realized that Hudson Grenbrier was a six foot five inch lamprey and he was sucking the talent out of his victims. Remembering what he looked like with his jaw unhinged and the circular rows of razor sharp teeth slashing through my flesh. Trena was right about him being far worse than any boogie man a child could conjure. Without fully opening my eyes I started scooting backwards across the floor towards the door, hoping Trena would continue to distract him. I made it to the hall when my slick sweaty palms slipped on the tile and I went down hard on my right elbow. I held my breath and listened. Footsteps. I definitely heard footsteps. While scrambling to my feet I caught a glimpse out of the corner of my eye. Hudson Greenbrier lunged towards me, jaw unhinged, and razor teeth gnashing. I jumped to one side to avoid being pummeled and Hudson stepped down hard where my sweaty palm had left a slick spot. He careened forward only stopping from the weight of his skull crashing into the doorframe. Hudson Greenbrier hit the floor with a thud. He was semiconscious but his mouth continued to hang open and the grotesque suction cup pulsed as though it was trying to feed.

Trena was at my side. "He is dazed. Now is our chance to end this for good." She ran back to the kitchen before I could say anything.

I looked down at this thing lying on the floor. Part human and part monster. He had been attacked by the lampreys and instead of draining him completely of his blood they had distorted his chemistry and left him with a super strength nose and the ability to drain talent. Maybe I was in an episode of the fucking X-Files. I rubbed my throbbing temples and leaned against the wall before I ended up falling on my all-time favorite writer.

Trena returned with a syringe. It was loaded with an opaque fluid. Before uncapping it she twisted the needle out and then she leaned down next to the gaping mouth. She took aim and squirted the fluid directly into the center of the pulsating suction cup. The thing started sputtering and squealing causing Hudson

Greenbrier to come to. He tried to speak but his unhinged jaw would not allow it. His massive hands reached out for me and if Trena had not pulled me aside in time he would have had me in his death grip once and for all. We held tight to each other and watched as the lamprey part of this man began to shrivel. After several moments the deafening squeal ceased as did the pulsating sucker. He was a whole man again nonetheless dead but whole. No one questioned the cause of death as being natural causes. Trena had only killed the lamprey. The true man had died long ago.

It had been lamprey poison in that syringe. Trena had acquired it in her travels with the author, but she had never been brave enough to use it until then. I was one lucky bastard. As for the trilogy that Hudson Greenbrier was working on, it did not exist. Trena told me that he had not written anything since the last novel was released. Once the man and monster were dead Trena regained her ability as a writer. And quite the writer she was. As for me, I'm still on top, if that's what you want to call it. Regardless of that, I am not immune to the occasional case of the jitters late at night when all should be quiet and is not.

The End.

CASE #: 20703

THE HANDSHAKE
BY CINDY O'QUINN

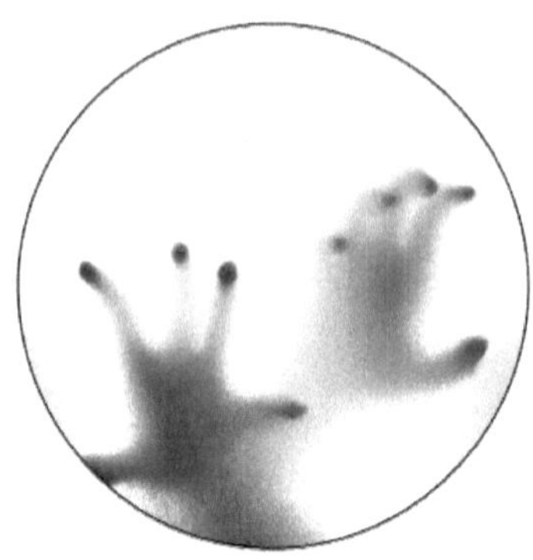

Cindy O'Quinn lives on an old homestead that is tucked away in the North Woods of New England, just a stones throw away from the Canadian border.

When she is not working on the homestead you can find her up in the loft of the log cabin writing stories.

Additional work of Cindy's can be found in upcoming issues of Blood Moon Rising Magazine.

Shelly Review by Heaven Of Horror

Scandinavian horror is on a roll with Shelley as a sinister addition to the New Nordic films – but don't worry, almost all the dialogue is in English.

There's so much beauty and light at the beginning of Shelley, but all that changes once you pay attention. The sounds and emotions portrayed are pretty grimm, which is in stark contrast to the lightness and beauty of the surroundings.

Also, there's an amazing relationship between the two main characters, Louise and Elena. Even though Elena is working for Louise, there's a clear sense of her being a part of the household. Louise has just had a miscarriage (and subsequently had to have a hysterectomy), so she truly needs help from Elena.

Elena is embracing the very strange living circumstances – out in the middle of a forrest, with no electricity or running water – but lets it be known that she thinks it's very strange. It's a wonderfully direct and honest communication, which means a mutual respect is quick to develop. Louise always wanted kids and hates that Elena has to be away from her son, so she offers Elena a quick way to earn a lot of money: Become a surrogate for Louise and her husband Kasper. Elena agrees and all is well, as the pregnancy is a success… but then every-thing changes.

Elena becomes very sick. She can't hold down food, finds it im-possible to sleep and keeps clawing at herself. She becomes convinced that whatever is in her womb, is trying to kill her. Louise is completely torn, as she battles with herself; She feels for the visible broken Elena, but also want her child to grow strong and be born. The way the story unfolds in Shelley is very elegant, and especially the visual style sup-ports this. From the carefree sun-filled days to the dark forces pulling at everyone involved.

I won't give away any more details, but I will say that a lot of the supporting characters are a big part of the story. Still, the characters of Louise and Elena carry the story and really, I loved every scene with them.

The light and beauty of the beginning turns downright sinister There's no doubt that the stars of Shelley are Ellen Dorrit Petersen (Louise) and Cosmina Stratan (Elena). Petersen is actually Nor-wegian – and speaks Norwegian in this movie (it irks me that everyone keeps saying they're a Danish married couple) – and starred in Blind from 2014, which was received extremely well and won a lot of awards. Romanian Cosmina Stratan is no stranger to awards either, as she won Best Actress at Cannes Film Festival in 2012 for Cristian Mungiu's Be-yond the Hills.

I was surprised to learn that Shelley is actually a feature film de-but for director, Ali Abbasi. Abbasi was born in Iran in 1981, but moved to Stockholm in 2002 and graduated from the Danish Film School in 2011. Shelley also features actors from both Denmark, Norway and Sweden along with Stratan from Romania, of course, so this is truly a cross-border project. The script for Shelley was written by Abbasi, as well, but in cooperation with Maren Louise Käehne, who has quite a few Danish successes (and awards) under her belt already.

This past year we've also had the zombie drama What We Be-come and are looking forward to the horror movie Finale, so things are finally looking up for New Nordic horror movies.

Shelley is out on VOD and limited release in the US, while still playing film festivals worldwide – including at FrightFestin the UK this month.

Details
Director: Ali Abbasi
Writer: Ali Abbasi, Maren Louise Käehne
Cast: Ellen Dorrit Petersen, Cosmina Stratan, Björn Andrésen,
Peter Christoffersen

ScreamQueen:

Sometimes a chosen name seems to stick, but it's no secret that my real name is Karina Adelgaard. I write reviews and recaps on HeavenofHorror.com and yes, it does happen that I find myself screaming, when watching a good horror movie. I love psychological horror, survival horror and kick-ass women. Also, I have a huge soft spot for a good horror-comedy. Oh yeah, and I absolutely HATE when animals are harmed in movies, so I will immediately think less of any movie, where animals are harmed for entertainment (even if the animals are just really good actors). Fortunately, horror doesn't use this nearly as much as comedy. And people assume horror lovers are the messed up ones. Go figure!

HorrorDiva:

My real name is Nadja Houmøller, but the name HorrorDiva
just seems to work for me. I usually keep up-to-date with all the
horror news, and make sure Heaven of Horror share the best
and latest trailers for upcoming horror movies. I love all kinds
of horror. My love affair started when I watched 'Poltergeist'
alone around the age of 10. I slept like a baby that night and I
haven't stopped watching horror movies since. The crazy
slasher stuff isn't really for me, but hey, to each their own. I
guess I just like to be scared and get jump scares, more than
being disgusted and laughing at the grotesque. Also, Korean
and Spanish horror movies made within the past 10-15 years are
among my absolute favorites.

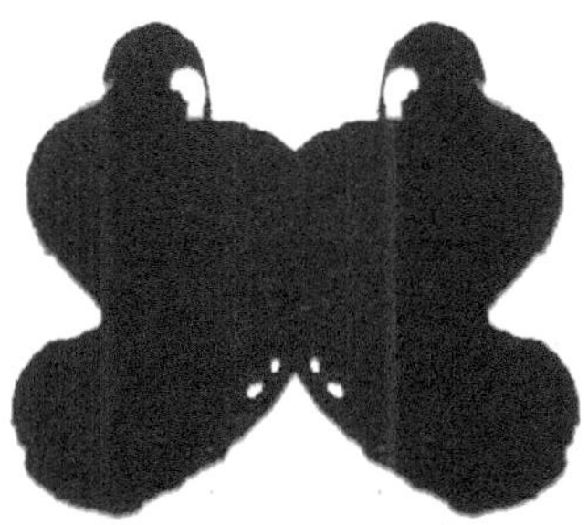

Of My Wounds, There Are Many by Stephanie M. Wytovich

Snapshot to blood and bone,

there's a knife in my head,

but my migraine was two years in the making, stitched to the

side of my skull like the arrow tip lodged behind my eye,

buried in my brain like the bruises of last night's thunder storm,

my teeth ripped from my mouth, shoved down my throat like

how the sky pushes out rain.

Of my wounds, there are many:

see the delicate stigmata cut into my hands and feet, the gashes

dug into my thighs, the tally-mark slashes on my wrists; I am

the punctured female, the pincushion of hysteria,

a traumatized sack of feminine injury, the flesh of my flesh, the

scar of my scar, I'm a collection of lesions and lacerations, a

patchwork of black and blue contusions worn out from where

you scrubbed me raw,

beat me till I seeped red like rare, woman steak.

Look to me on this table as I bleed and break,
a toy of operation, a surgical muse to the amputation of

bodily consciousness: hear me when I say I feel nothing, that

with each incision and penetration, I am dead,

gone from this world of torment and torture, a

disappearance, an acceptance to oblivion, to the land

where I can forget the flower, the blossom of what I saw

lies underneath.

Yes, use my soon-to-be-corpse as a nametag,

as a placard to the other girls who are destined to bleed;

I am closing my eyes to your knives now, deafening myself

to the fractures you inflict; I will cease to be your canvas of

mutilation, Only a head, a torso, a heart,

best to photograph me while in transition; it's the last chance

you'll have to locate my soul.

CASE #: 46596

OF MY WOUNDS, THERE ARE MANY
BY STEPHANIE M. WYTOVICH

Stephanie M. Wytovich is an instructor by day and a horror writer by night. She is the Poetry Editor for Raw Dog Screaming Press, an adjunct at Western Connecticut State University, and a book reviewer for Nameless Magazine. She is a member of the Science Fiction Poetry Association, an active member of the Horror Writers Association, and a graduate of Seton Hill University's MFA program for Writing Popular Fiction. Her Bram Stoker Award-nominated poetry collections, Hysteria: A Collection of Madness, Mourning Jewelry, An Exorcism of Angels, and Brothel can be found at www.rawdogscreaming.com, and her debut novel, The Eighth, is to be published through Dark Regions Press. Follow Wytovich at stephaniewytovich.com and on twitter @JustAfterSunset

Hello horror lover.
If you've been suffering from a persistent desire
for just a little more unpleasantness in your life,
we have the answer:
NOCTURNAL
TRANSMISSIONS
PODCAST
Nocturnal Transmissions is a fortnightly podcast featuring
inspired performances of dark tales both old and new
by voice artist Kristin Holland.
Find them at
nocturnaltransmissions.com.au
or wherever good podcasts are purveyed.

If you have any feedback or would like to leave a review please head over to Amazon and share your thoughts about Sanitarium.

Thank you for your time and we salute your love for all things horror.

https://www.facebook.com/SanitariumPublishing

https://www.thesanitarium.co.uk/

https://twitter.com/sanitariumlit

https://www.instagram.com/sanitariumpublishing/